Acknowledgements

John Skipp would mostly like to thank all the intrepid, batshit-crazy souls who labor inside the motion picture industry: not just in Hollywood, but all over the world. On behalf of all of us who love movies – even bad ones – almost more than life itself, this painfully comical fuckoid love song of hope and doom is for you.

Special thanks to blood family, heart family, film family, art family, horror and Bizarro family.You all know who you are. Extra-specials for Andrew Kasch, my other art brother; Jane Hamilton, Scooby Hamilton, and all the residents of Cazador Manor; Creative Underground Los Angeles; the village of Los Feliz; the women of the Viscera Film Festival; Scott Bradley; Rose O'Keefe; LitReactor; Fangoria; the Jumpcut Cafe; and half the peeps and places Cody's about to mention.

Cody Goodfellow would like to thank all the people who work every day to make sure this book never comes true. Also, everyone who makes Los Angeles the irradiated wasteland we know and sometimes love: Rob Winfield, Lisa Morton, RL Grove, Bob Johnson, Dan Weinstein, Morgan Bazinet, John Palisano, Chris Farnsworth, Iliad Bookshop, Dark Delicacies, the Warner Grand Theater, HP Lovecraft Historical Society, Hyaena Gallery, House Of Secrets, Pickwick Bowl, Echo/Echoplex, Copy Hub Ray, KCRW, Museum of Jurassic Technology, Chili John's, Killer Shrimp, Not A Burger Stand, Irwin's Conspiracy, Aaron Vanek, Darius Shahmir, Benji Gillespie,Victoria Goodfellow and Cassius.

For our daughters.

THE LAST GODDAM HOLLYWOOD MOVIE

JOHN SKIPP & CODY GOODFELLOW

ILLUSTRATIONS BY GREG HOUSTON

In the last film I ever saw
They wore suits and they wore ties
In the last film I ever saw
They kept the change and they told lies

—*"The Last Film"* by Kissing The Pink

1
Establishing Shots

The first red rays of dawn wring blood from the clouds over Santa Catalina Island. Our hero and sole survivor, PETER KORNBERG, strolls through the ruins of the town of Avalon to sit at the head of Green Pier with his camera in one hand, and an hourglass containing the island's last ounce of unirradiated cocaine in the other.

The black bay still burns in patches where fuel leaked out of the island's sunken yacht armada. None of the villas and shops facing the harbor stand tall enough to feed a fire, but the gutted casino off to his left burns merrily on, a huge gray-black tower of smoke leaning to curl an accusing finger at the rising sun, and the blasted wasteland of North America.

I can't direct myself, let alone act, for shit. My name is Peter Kornberg, and I am a recovering liar. I am writing this to tell the truth.

The prevailing ocean wind kept the worst of the fallout from reaching us for six blessed months. It's a miracle we survived as long as we did. There were refugees and pirates, but Avalon was not merciless, nor defenseless. The big 70mm artillery on the headland never fired a shot at the ones who burned us to the ground until it was too late.

I check my hat—the peak of the brittle white straw Stetson is chopped open where a piece of shrapnel narrowly missed my brains. Lucky hat, stained by red rain and the darker dapples of someone else's blood.

The black sticks scattered around the dead bonfires along Casino Way are not wood. I shot enough footage of the barbecue, got close enough that the stink will never come out of my hair and clothes.

They took all the women. They cooked and ate all the men, the living and the dead. As thorough as if they drilled

11

for it, they left nothing for the gulls.

I should bury them. I should erect a shrine, a monument, and compose a noble epitaph. They didn't fall like the Spartans, and nobody would go to heaven following in their footsteps. If they had anything worth passing on to the future, it was their good fucking luck, while it lasted.

But once, they made movies and sang songs and wrote books, and they tried to keep the torch lit.

A younger Kornberg would have carved something, if only an angry THEY DESERVED BETTER on the pedestal of the statue overlooking the bay. But Kornberg at 45 has no words, and can not even cry.

***

I quit writing poetry in college, and built an enviable career writing scripts for movies I sincerely believed in. Nice work if you can get it. Many came, but few were chosen.

I was holed up in Zane Gray's cabin on Paramount's tab—strapped for a second act to a serious Oscar-bait melodrama—when L.A. detonated, and the radios went crazy, and the superheated pyroclastic clouds rolled over the island like a magic wand.

When the dust settled, the streets of Avalon were littered with roasted corpses, haunted by shrieking survivors who wasted away in days. I helped with the dying, listened to the garbled bits of news from the mainland, and went to a party that lasted a week. Then I went home and burned my script.

I'd avoided the news while I was writing, but it didn't matter how it happened, any more than it mattered all the times it almost happened. The men in power had fallen down on the job, and now there were no more countries, because some assholes believed lies some other assholes told them, that they could do it and survive, that they could win. And the world had let them make such awful weapons and whip them around the global stage like big prosthetic dicks, because the world was drunk on the hail Mary happy ending lies Hollywood told them.

No more lies.

I haven't seen another survivor since I came out of my hole in the hills. The war hit at high season, but there were fewer than a thousand residents, and three hundred visitors. Another fifty or so came along after, in lonely sailboats, yachts, the Coast Guard cutter… and the Chinese freighter, but never mind that.

Most of the island's defenders were sitting shivva at Masada, Avi Sobel's compound above Cabrillo Mole, when the attack came. Sobel's reformed Jewish grief cult was a huge drag, but they fought like tigers with the arsenal he'd built up from his cheap action movies. A salvo of missiles erased his fortress. Sobel let his pretensions go to his head, and passed out cyanide.

Most of the island had come down to the harbor to greet them. The news spread like a case of crabs, and everyone who wasn't dead drunk or praying to an Israeli film producer gathered on Casino Way. The harbormaster had received and acknowledged a hail and request to enter port with serial numbers and spit and polish on it.

The raiders searched the island and rooted out everything with a heat profile, then came back to feast and flatten the town. And like that first lethal heatwave, they left with the wind.

I was there with my camera. I have it all on tape.

Not that it matters anymore…

At least that's what I'm thinking when something solid and shiny winks in the ruddy sunlight, out beyond the mouth of the bay.

***

I stand and strain to see what slides out of the smoke into the harbor against the smoking tide. No masts or pilothouse break the haze, but a low, long profile plows the water in dirty New York snow waves. For a moment, I believe I see a whale.

Sergei the sound guy, who used to carry his Oscar around

as a club, took over the marine biology gear on the backside of the island. He recorded the nightmare-choirs of whole pods of gray whales dying in the first week, then nothing.

I fire up my camera and zoom in on it.

The last whale coming here to die would almost ruin the mood—too on the nose—but the viewfinder shows me a sleek, overgrown dorsal fin with men standing in it. Déjà vu, post-trauma flashback tremors. They're looking at me through binoculars and a camera. One of them zooms in on me taping them. None of them points a gun.

I figure they can see my middle finger well enough.

Maybe these assholes got lost on their way to our *Pirates of the Caribbean* reenactment, or maybe they're just some whole other assholes. For all I care, they could be the real Navy, hot on the trail of the fuckers who raped and pillaged Avalon. This would be a perfect ending, better than the anticlimactic starvation death scripted for me. They could shoot me down and cook me, but someone, someday, would find the camera and the disks in the bag on my hip, and they would know the truth.

But nobody shoots. A Zodiac raft with three men in it pops out of the submarine and buzzes across the bay to idle alongside the half-submerged wreckage of the pier.

"Top of the morning, Pete!" A short man draped in a billowing poncho hails me through a bullhorn. The flat metallic slap of his bright, cheery voice echoes off the ruins at my back.

I can't see the man's face, but the dripping red beard under his billed captain's hat gives him away. In the world before the Day, only a handful of people could truly seem worth the karmic damage of hoping for their death, but producer Julian Harvey was one of them.

"Of all the people I hoped I might find alive, you were on top of my list!" Harvey squawks as one of the pair of able-bodied seamen climbs out onto the charred pier and lashes the raft to a concrete piling. "I told Shahmir this morning, if anyone's got the wits to see this through, it'll be Kornberg."

The sailor comes up to me and stops with his hands in

the pockets of his peacoat. I zoom in on his studiously blank face. The hourglass will make a shitty weapon. Too bad I never won an Oscar, like Sergei. "I don't have any food, Harvey. And I probably have AIDS, so raping or eating me would be stupid."

Harvey cracks up, overloading the bullhorn. He puts it down and shouts, "Fantastic, that's hilarious. You can joke, so you're probably still sane. Good, great. Come onboard, man. I want to talk to you."

The raiders sank every boat that they didn't take with them. I was planning to go up in the hills to snort the coke, gibber and tweak until I had a heart attack or got morose enough to jump in the sea with my pockets full of rocks. Catalina is a dead island. And God is a hack, if he let Julian Harvey escape.

"What do you want from me?"

"I was hoping we could have lunch and talk on the sub, but if you're going to be a dick about it, I wonder if you might be looking for work."

"I worked in the bakery and took my turns on harbor patrol. You find a new island with a live town, and I'll bake their bread."

"There's nowhere else to go, Pete. This... it's sad, but you survived it. You're double-lucky, and if your work meant anything, it matters now, more than ever."

If there was any other living soul to take up with, insane, cannibal or otherwise, I would walk. But Julian's talking like the raid never happened, like the bombs never dropped. Some of the craziest people on the island talked like that, in deluded loops, like this was all just a grueling shoot, like the world was still out there.

I repeat myself. "What do you want from me, Julian?"

"I want you to come with us. We're going back to America to make a movie."

My laughter is like a bloodied animal escaping from a trap. "You're fucking insane."

Harvey shrugs, but his lackey clenches up, about to strike. "No, I'm doing what I do, Pete. So long as I live,

15

I'll make movies. What are you going to do, with however many hours or days you have left? Come with us. Live a little longer, and do one more picture. America needs it."

"America is dead, Harvey!"

"Not a bit of it! She's down, and she's bleeding, but she'll rise up. Never dead, Pete. Don't say that."

Harvey stands awkwardly in the raft. Behind his pretentious hornrim glasses, his eyes look like they're tearing up. "I have actors and a crew. I have equipment, and I have supplies. I even have a decent caterer. All I need is a genius to make it happen."

"I meant what I said, Harvey. Whatever happened to the rest of the world, so long as I'm alive, I'm never working with you again."

"Oh for Christ's sake, get in the boat! I'm trying to be a better me, when it's never been easier to be worse."

"You'd kidnap me?"

"Kidnapping? Pete, they ate our friends and neighbors!"

"So that makes whatever you do kosher?"

"You're still mad about the *Indian Giver* deal. That's kind of mental, but I understand pride. You think yours is bigger than the whole world, but I'm big enough to swallow mine, to show you that you're wrong. Tell you what, I saved the best for last."

"If it gets any better, just kill me now."

"I want you to direct."

I swallow my next words. This calls for reevaluation. I didn't survive, and this is Rod Serling's hell.

"Get in the goddamned boat, already!"

The sailor helps me down the ladder of debris and into the raft. Harvey points at my backpack. "Is that your only luggage?"

"Just the camera and my disks. I shot the island the entire time. I've got hours of raw footage, interviews with everyone..."

"That's wonderful, really. No, I mean... Is *that* what I think it is?" He points at the hourglass.

It came from Avi Sobel's bunker. Avi saved the last

ounce from the marathon orgy that gripped the island in the first month, and recast it as a totem of their lost lives. I never had much of a taste for the stuff, but figured it'd serve as currency, or a last, stupid fling, if there's enough of it to kill me.

Harvey signals a sailor, who takes it from me. "You're a godsend, Pete, and this from a devout atheist. I was starting to worry about how I was going to keep my crew happy, once the vodka ran out."

2
Pre-Production

The brainstorming session turns out to be a pitch, and a ceremonial one at that, but I listen passively until the end. "Fuck you. Keep the coke, but let me out."

"It's not negotiable anymore, Pete." Harvey's smiling eyes semaphore furiously, *not in front of the crew*. He moves to take me out of the galley by my arm.

I shake free. "Stop. I know you're all in shock, right now. I loved everyone on that island like a family, too. I want to honor their memory, too. That's why I don't understand how he's got you all sold on this insane bullshit project."

I look around the galley stuffed with faces, grubby, ash-black hands clutching the bottled water and cartons of Silk Cut 100's Harvey passed out. Many I knew quite well from Catalina, some I worked with in Hollywood. Good people, smart and talented... and balanced.

An ugly suspicion spikes my hair-trigger bullshit-detector, which a lifetime of dealing with producers has inflamed into a lobe of its own in my brain. These aren't just refugees. They are a crew, hand-picked. Sobel's cult weeded out the kooks and the insecure, and the raid claimed everyone with enough guts to fight, but I find it hard to believe Harvey trawled the island for survivors and magically assembled this group. "So, how long has this piece of shit been in development hell, anyway?"

Marina speaks up, her Slavic accent bristling for maximum effect. Ten years younger than me, Harvey's director of photography got nominated for three Oscars, a host of awards in Europe. "We didn't plan any of this before our home was destroyed... again..." The crew mumbles assent. "This isn't another suicide cult, but we don't just want to survive. We want to work."

19

"Well, it *is* suicide to go back there, and a pipe dream to try to make a film. L.A. is a crater. There is no *there* anymore! And the story… even if you could shoot a film and edit it, and find enough survivors who want to take time out of their slow, agonizing deaths to watch it, why make up a whopper of a lie like that?"

"What did we ever do," Harvey smirks, "but tell lies? You can't tell people the truth straight out. People don't like to feel stupid or guilty. Your films always had a genius about slipping in a long, thin knife, Pete. Your lies hurt like the truth, but that didn't make them true."

"I documented Avalon, the whole six months. I wasn't partying with you guys that night, because I was down at the harbor. I saw who did that to us, and I know some of you did, too. Lies killed our country, didn't they? Maybe the world."

"Bullshit," cries the Greek chorus. "Sure, blame Hollywood. Maybe Oliver Stone pushed the button. Throw him off the boat…"

"Listen, Pete," Harvey gathers his wind, reining in his temper as his face flushes red to match his beard, "you want to tell everyone the truth about what happened, fine. Kick the survivors in the teeth. There's already enough bitterness to power a city on this boat right now."

He turns to take in all those faces, then pivots to focus all their pathos on me like a lens, like a lawyer pleading for their lives.

"The world has fallen down, true. All the big cities are gone. All our friends and family, all the people and places we loved have been erased. The ones who lived through it are fighting against a perfectly natural despair. Even if they can feed themselves and find shelter and clean water, they won't be any better than animals if they stop believing in the big lie that civilization carried on for the last thousand years.

"They need a new mythology. If they're going to beat the despair that's eating them up, they need to see somebody take responsibility for what they did, and repent of it, and try to make the world a better place. That's the truth, isn't it, Pete?"

"You want to take the man who stepped over the body of our President—"

"An everyman, thrust into a situation already out of control—"

"He was a callow, bloodthirsty douchebag, and probably the patsy for a coup! Installing him at the last minute was as good as pushing the button. And you know what people say. Nobody from outside the government could have gotten to the President and the VP at the same time…"

"Nobody knows for sure how it happened. We all heard the radio. Some said they hit us first, and some say it was an inside job. But that's not the story we're going to tell. The truth about that won't help anybody right now. We take one man…"

"Not him, anyone but him…"

"He's already cast. And we follow him as he witnesses what his policies did, and he takes all of it onto his shoulders…"

"And he finds the ring of power, and turns into Jesus, flies backwards around the world and undoes Armageddon. Does anybody else need a bucket to throw up in?"

Harvey herds me into a corner, whispers in my ear, "*It's going to happen, okay?* Not negotiable. It's going to happen.

"You know, I was a mean motherfucker when I made films for money. Well, I'm not making this for money. I'm making it so maybe a movie might actually do what we used to lie to ourselves they could do, and save the fucking world. And maybe a better berth in Hell, which I'm already resigned to, atheist that I am.

"I want you to write this film and direct it, but nobody is going to stand in its way, do you understand me?"

Something jabs me in the gut. I'm afraid to look down. If anyone would stab me in front of a roomful of witnesses, it's Julian Harvey.

"Okay," I surrender. "Give me the fucking notes. I didn't see any gear onboard, so I'm assuming you'll need my camera, too?"

Harvey grins. "Oh, I've got cameras. And a whole lot more. So get ready to use 'em.

"We start shooting an hour and a half from now."

3
Casting

Of our cast to date, I quickly learn, only six are actors by trade. The rest fill out shots as sailors or extras or whatever, but each had to pick up another skill, usually a shit survival job no union crew would ever stoop to.

So there are no perfumed ten-million dollar princesses in our ragged troupe. It's like Boxing Day, all year round.

I wonder if Harvey even auditioned them before he let them come aboard his submarine—bought entirely, he tells me, with overseas profits from *The Indian Giver*.

Which is where all of our bad blood went down...

***

The Indian Giver—so hilariously named, in retrospect, that you'd think I'd have seen it coming—was my big shot at a studio feature I might actually get to direct. After years of hustling, and helming a couple of no-pay indie features, I delivered the script to Dreamworks, who loved it, and wound up promising me the chair.

Harvey took it from me, booted my ass off the film in the third day of shooting, turned it into an action picture, and made a fortune. $236 mil in its opening weekend. $1.3 *billion* worldwide, by the time the world caved in.

Sure, I got sweet residuals from my one-third-of-the-script and "Based On A Story By" credits, but it thoroughly destroyed me personally. Getting fired by Harvey essentially killed my directorial career, ripped the tits off my marriage, and sent me spiraling for several years.

Adding insult to injury was this one inescapable fact: the movie I wrote would have won festival award noms and critical drool, but it wouldn't have bought me a Starbucks croissant, much less the cup of latte it rode in on.

Meanwhile, he buys a submarine. Which just happens to come in handy, here at the end of the world.

So he was right and I was wrong, if right equals might and wrong equals simple human decency.

And clearly, that's the new math.

But it's not like Harvey to leave anything that eats, shits, or accrues billable hours idling in limbo. And he's not a writer, just a conceptualizer.

So he fobs off the other characters, and how they'll be played, on me.

"It's a road movie. We'll figure out who they are, and find the rest on the road.

"Meanwhile, start dreaming. Then I'll take you to meet your star."

***

Over the next hour, I puzzle over the notes, written to Harvey's exacting specifications (EXPECT SURPRISES), before we're brought topside and prepped for landing. Thirty-five of us are about to be dressed in sailors' and marines' uniforms, stuffed into five rafts, then unleashed on the mainland California beach.

And there he is, perched over the rail.

Charlie Beecher—as Defense Secretary Ellison Boyle—wears a tattered charcoal gray Brooks Brothers suit. His once-distinguished John Forsythe face is nearly as tattered and gray as the suit, and his vomit overpowers the dead ocean funk with the reek of pure cognac.

"You've got to be fucking kidding me!" I shout in Harvey's ear. It's loud above deck.

Harvey rolls his eyes. "He's had a solid career..."

"Yeah, on prime time soaps...!"

"Playing senators, oil men, people of power..."

"Yeah! ON SHITTY PRIME TIME SOAPS...!"

"You know he did good work in film, for Sid Lumet and Coppola."

"C'mon, Harvey! That was thirty years ago. And in case you forgot, he hasn't worked in ten. And he's not just mediocre. He's a scary-ass fucking drunk!"

Harvey cocks an eyebrow worthy of Mothra as he refills my empty glass. "You got a problem with drunks, you're on the wrong boat."

"Jesus! Beecher didn't just have a sloppy DUI! He jumped a curb on Doheny and hit people. People with lawyers."

"How many people did he kill?"

"What's that got to do with…?"

"Less than six billion, though, right?"

Though I start to sputter, it stops me in my tracks.

"Look at him," Harvey continues. I helplessly do. Beecher ralphs a little more of his signature fragrance over the rail. "He's a broken man, yearning for one last chance. So he's already typecast. And you can't deny the resemblance."

It's true. Watching him, I can't help but wish that the *real* Ellison Boyle were this miserable and pathetic right now. If wishes were fishes, and we had either of them left, I would snap his neck and toss him over the side in a thermoflash second.

So I guess it's perfect casting, after all.

4
Action

When we disembark from the submarine in a flotilla of Zodiac rafts, the natives are waiting for us. They pour down out of the canyons in the concrete cliffs of downtown Long Beach, backdropped by a jigsaw jumble of pulverized skyscrapers.

I hunker down behind the pontoons like the biggest pussy at Normandy on D-Day. Thirty-five of us stuffed into five rafts, dressed like sailors and marines. Everyone wears a life jacket and helmet except Harvey and his Praetorian guards, who wear flak jackets. I wonder if Harvey can swim.

I clear my throat and shout, "Action!"

Our gallant lead leans over the edge and pukes into the surf. Marina zooms in.

I try to direct Marina, but I'm out of my depth keeping up with her. She climbs onto the outer pontoons to frame Boyle's first glimpse of the new America. His ashen nausea perfectly crystallizes the view.

The natives charge down to the edge of the surf. Arrows, spears and homemade lawn darts impale the waves. The swells lift and drop us ten feet as the rafts carve through the dirty white breakers.

The lead raft capsizes on the face of a shockingly big wave. Harvey shouts orders over me and my puny bullhorn, but I can at least watch the second camera feed on the souped-up Palm Pilot Harvey gave me: panning across the gauntlet of savages hurling death and curses at us.

They all have starved, Dachau-skinny bodies clad in rags and mud and bits of scavenged regalia from the old world. Perfectly cast for Skull Island, except most of them are blonde.

Our raft heels back on a lull and shoots the rolling trough between two rearing waves. Marina rolls back into the

raft as a spear flicks through the frame and punctures the starboard pontoon. I shout, "Cut!" but Harvey roars, "KEEP SHOOTING!"

In the raft behind us, the sailors open fire with their rifles. The second unit captures the shooters silhouetted against the white fog. Marina turns to lens the shore. Before we turn into the wave, I see a native on the beach do a backflip with a red blur for a face.

"Cut! Cut! He's shooting real bullets–" but nobody hears. Our raft plows up onto the shore. The sailors leap out and drag the raft up onto the pebbles just ahead of the next gnashing wave. An instant intern, I jump out and try to help.

The flipped raft wallows in the breakers. A few heads pop up in the shallows and try to find their feet. The second unit frames our cook, whom I remember was named Saul, catching an arrow in his teeth. He flops and rolls over in the surf. Harry Walter, our editor, tries to lift him up, but a flurry of spears rain on him, and he dives out of sight. Harvey screams with genuine worry at Walter to stay down.

Like landscapers watering a lawn, the sailors mow down the natives in lazy autofire arcs. Most of the shots go over their heads, and maybe the magazines are half-blanks, because they only kill three of the dozens of hungry barbarians. The rest retreat back up the canyons, setting off miniature landslides, turning to hurl darts and final curses that have almost no meaning to me. Maybe nobody speaks English anymore.

The rest of the rafts beach without incident, and the wounded are dragged onto shore. Saul is DOA, and his rescuer took a shallow wound to the shoulder. Marina keeps shooting.

I drift over to the nearest corpse. A naked boy of about fourteen, with too little of his face left for me to judge any more. Naked, that is, but for a tight pink T-shirt that looks brand new against his filthy, slat-ribbed carcass. CATALINA JUNIOR LIFEGUARD, the T-shirt says. Round his narrow waist, an olive drab military surplus belt with a bellows pouch. It's stuffed with Twinkies.

Beecher wanders over and kneels beside the corpse of an emaciated woman, belly gravid with hunger, sunken chest cracked open and smoking. Marina hovers, spinning gold from the leaden moment.

"I want a burial detail," Beecher shouts. A sailor laughs at him and takes the dead boy's Twinkies.

***

I want to go over and talk to Harvey, but I'm drowned out by the sound of helicopters.

Two Chinooks and an Apache gunship clear the cliffs by inches and drop down onto the shore. Spraypainted over the flags and serial numbers: DAMAGE, INC., JESUS LOVES YOU and SEMPER FOR HIRE.

Marina and Dieter, the second camera, weave through the chaotic landfall like it's been storyboarded for months. I dance back to stay out of the frame. Harvey mutely directs his goons with hand signals. They flatten the rafts and stack the gear.

A bull-necked Marine lieutenant in full body armor jogs out of the propwash hurricane to shake Harvey's hand. More jarheads with sharp, fresh haircuts and spotless uniforms make short work of the gear.

Before I can yell, "Cut!" again, the whole boating party is stowed away on the Chinooks, while the Apache hovers out over the water with its machine guns swiveling back and forth.

Expect Surprises, indeed.

5
Technical Support

Colonel Dalrymple says he had a vision, the day before the bombs. Jesus told him to pull his company out of desert maneuvers and take shelter in borax mines stocked with civil defense supplies. So he did.

When they emerged, he and his righteous God Warriors were the only Marines left.

D Company was stationed at Camp Pendleton, but the radiation from the San Onofre meltdown makes the Geiger counters growl, so they winter near the old Air Corps base at Twenty-Nine Palms.

The choppers beat across the broken coast, pivot inland over Anaheim through flurries of Disneyland ash. Black steel Matterhorn skeletons rear up out of carpets of cinders undisturbed by the least little sign of life.

"What am I in charge of?" I demand.

Harvey hands me a clipboard, introduces me to my line producer. A sleepy-eyed Persian guy with a righteous utility belt pumps my hand, something-Shahmir, and starts force-feeding me raw data.

I push past Shahmir to collar Harvey, yukking it up with the pilots in their bugeyed helmets. "If this turns into a snuff film, one of us is going to star in it before it's over."

Harvey nods thoughtfully, shouts back in my ear. "Fair enough. But why did we always fake it, in the old days?"

The old days. Civilization, humankind, reduced to a nasal dismissal, like wide ties and westerns. "Exploitation of suffering—"

Harvey crows, "Suffering! We exploit everything but the real on-camera death. Suffering put my kids through college…" He pauses, grins. "We've got two of the top five ILM pixel-crunchers onboard, Pete. You want to show only

31

fake death, fine… but they'll be up from here to opening night painting out all of that."

Harvey points at the highway below. From horizon to brimstone horizon, eight lanes of gridlocked traffic lie packed in beds of ash like forgotten toys rusting in the factory, or piled in heaps like dead roaches, where cyclonic firestorms from the bombs swept them aside.

"Yeah, have Bao and Rob see to that," Harvey smirks. "I'd hate for critics to say I descended into exploitation filmmaking."

6
Location

The desert shrinks us to scuttling insects, dung beetles rolling a monument of manure across the infinite gray plain to the feet of the towering pagan idol of Lord Julian Harvey.

The dust and glowing sand roar night and day over the empty earth; ghostly monoliths of granite and gutted concrete and Joshua trees and here and there, the drifting ghosts, weightless as tumbleweeds. The few survivors that pass within sight seem to know, to come no closer. Even in this empty, dark afterlife, I guess word gets around.

Dust sifts through our masks (black outside, red inside), makes deserts of our mouths, lungs and eyes.

Even in the dank crypts of the bunkers, the dust drifts on the triple-filtered air. Hacking coughs punctuate every conversation.

Marina can hold her breath like a pearl diver, and makes it obvious why losers invented steadicams and dollies.

Meanwhile, Beecher slowly melts down, totally digested by Ellison Boyle. I throw him lines off the top of my head, and he hurls them back up as madness: semi-digested curds of jingo, platitude, compassion, regret, and rage.

A boy who lives off the camp's trash adopts him, following him and reacting to his raving with caws and barks and howls. He reminds me of the Feral Kid from *The Road Warrior*, only more heartbreaking, because it's all organic. There is no acting going on here. Only total, pristine insanity.

I let the two of them run amok, try to imagine what I'm actually in control of here.

The answer, clearly, is nothing.

How can I possibly plot a story that mutates every time we turn around? And what does "directing" even mean, when every moment is spent just scrambling to keep up with the changes?

All that said: *something* is definitely taking shape here. Some weird post-nuke inversion of "docu-drama", wherein you make up a narrative, then let the history of the moment-by-moment show you how it all plays out.

Meanwhile, Harvey dispenses his own daily notes. His Master's Voice does not seem to adapt to the changing terrain, but to dictate it, as if this ruined world is all accounted for in the fx budget.

***

Well into the first week of shooting, the cast starts to take real shape, as well. Pierre Sinard, our costume and makeup specialist, has never acted in a film at all, but he does the best impression of Dalrymple, so he plays a thinly fictionalized take on the camp commander.

The marines of Damage, Inc. are eager to help: from location scouting to portraying Beecher's bodyguards, which they play with unflagging *Ooo-RAH!* gusto. Nobody ever sees one of them sleeping. The company runs on a supply of industrial speed designed for recon patrols and fighter pilots. Up for a week straight, they sleep a day in a closet with a boombox blasting Slayer.

For a scene where Boyle interrupts two marines' rape of a civilian refugee, they produced a bony slip of a girl as if from a pantry: a brunette to the bleached tips of her stringy, patchy hair where skunk-like stripes still ran from her bangs to her flea-infested crown. Her unblinking eyes like a tragic Keane painting, big glistening question marks, asking WHY?

They played the rape to the hilt, stopping each take just after ripping away her shapeless rag-frock to bare her unnervingly full bosom—I wondered if, wandering across the desert, it ever occurred to her to drink her fake boobs.

They pushed only so far as I ordered, and took delight in making me spell out their motivations and marks. They took the Secretary's arthritic caning ("You will respect this lady's DIGNITY!" he howls at the moment *of rapus interruptus*) with stoic good humor. The sergeant's jaunty wink at the prone, exhausted Boyle was a slice of heaven. When I vote for the Oscars this year, I'll write both of them in.

Dalrymple never says no, but he keeps an exacting tab. Every minute of labor is clocked; every soiled sheet, bottle of water, bowel-blocking MRE pouch, and every missed morning prayer service is tabulated. I have no idea what currency we will have to use to pay for it.

7
Working With Kids and Animals

One morning, Marina and I follow Beecher as he tries to crawl through the barbed wire and escape the camp. The feral boy slips through the wires without snagging his rags, but Secretary Boyle gets tangled up, unable to go forward or back, and panics. Very drunk. Seizure. The boy laughs and claps. Marina keeps rolling.

I beg her not to waste footage on schmaltz. I blunder into the wire to try to help, but then I panic. I hear barking. It isn't the boy.

A pack of wild dogs bounds out of the perpetual sandstorm. Marina captures zooming flashes of their mangy, naked hides, weeping sores, fibrous tumors like cauliflower, oozing eyes, and gnashing, foam-flecked teeth.

Secretary Boyle rages, daring them to come, even as he dared America's enemies. I scream cut, shredding my gloves and fingers on the barbed wire. Dogs converge on Boyle's trapped form and, one by one, press close to lick his face.

Then they turn on the boy and eat him.

When it's over, Marina stalks back toward the bunker with the camera. Hoarse and breathless, I shinny out of my tattered fatigues and leave Beecher weeping in the wire.

"Bitch! Stop and drop it, you fucking vulture!"

She keeps walking, but she must be screaming through her mask and over the wind. "You should thank God I shot it, Peter! Nothing in your so-called script could tell the story half so well as that!"

"Is that the kind of movie you wanted to make? Does that make you feel like a serious filmmaker? Maybe they still give out the Palm D'Or, who knows?"

"Is this about Beecher's acting, or George's?" Marina whirls on me. I duck, thinking she intends to brain me with

the camera. Naked eyes brimming with tears, caked with ash.

"Who?"

"George... the boy. Beecher took to... he liked to be called George." Marina peels off her gasmask. "I had a son named Alexander. I missed his last birthday party to do some underwater reshoots for a goddamned music video on Catalina, and he went to bed and never woke up."

"I had two boys, Marina. I don't know..." Choked up. "But they're probably dead. But we can't, can we? Use that moment. You were at Avalon..."

"I certainly was, Peter. And I had a man there, at the end. His name was Dennis. You probably didn't know him. He was an investment banker."

I bite back a protest that I taped everyone on the island, but I can't picture a banker named Dennis, let alone one who could tame Marina, the indie cinema tigress. "We did not talk about it, but we tried to have a baby. My period wouldn't stop, but the doctor said..." Choke. "He went down to the harbor to protect a woman he hadn't even made a baby with yet."

Marina looks down at the camera. The Cyclops glow of the replay makes neon streams of her tears. "If he were truly that man he's playing, I would have killed him myself. I saw what you saw at Avalon. It's a small world. And the script is shit, isn't it?"

I chuckle and nod, offer Marina a pint of Stoli the Marines never got to bill us for.

She gratefully bites off the cap and slugs hard, without coughing. Her eyes blush, red trees under glass, and her nose almost sizzles, but she doesn't puke. "Death for that fucker. I'm not such a nice lady, even for a Russian, you know? But if I were wiser, I would want him to know how my boy died on his birthday. Make him see it, not so? I wish somebody could have been there to film Alexander's death."

She digs in her bottomless bellows pockets and hands me a pair of wire cutters. "Get our leading man out before the dogs change their minds about diseased meat."

I start to leave, grateful to be dismissed, but then turn

back and stick my foot back in the trap. "What kind of film did you want to make, Marina?"

She laughs now, swaying, suddenly besotted with weeks of fatigue and half-buried grief. "Why should I do your job for you? Is my job to shoot the hell out of film, whatever it is. Stop asking people that, it freaks them out. You're supposed to be in charge."

"Harvey's in charge."

"God and the Devil are in charge, and they both owe Harvey favors. Go."

8
Rehearsal

She leaves me to stumble back along the perimeter. A hump of dust in the midst of the snarled wire turns over and shakes itself off. Beecher, naked and bleeding, trembles at my feet like a whipped dog.

Had I been about to kick him? It certainly crosses his mind, every time the poor fucker locks eyes with me.

Beecher takes it as his due, channels it into his method acting. The bellicose civilian Pentagon despot is long gone. When I watch the dailies of Beecher shot on the sub, I ache with pity and more than a little awe. From that first day to this, day eight of the shoot, Beecher looks like the before & after portraits of an embattled wartime president.

Beecher recites the President's final address like a terminal rosary, pours dust over his head like a spastic baptism. Naked but for the dust caked on his blood. His clothes hang on the wire like a smashed gray Brooks Brothers kite. He sheds them and crawls naked out of the wire, just like the feral boy showed him. Very little of the blood on him is his own.

I lead Beecher back to the bunker. The naked old man slouches against me, and has to be caught by his hand when I shove him off.

"Are you in there, Ellison Boyle? Is that you, Mr. Secretary?"

"God help me, for I stand at the brink of the pit, but I—"

"Shut up." I take Boyle's wattled neck in my fist. It shouldn't feel so good, so right. I shouldn't hear the whole world begging me to avenge it. "I hate you, Ellison Boyle. You killed our goddamned country." It feels good, indeed.

Punching him in the face feels even better.

"I know," Beecher croaks.

I hit him again.

41

Then shock myself by hugging him quickly, just before his knees give in. Keep him from hitting the ground, as he sobs against me, until he gathers his legs beneath him. And pray there are no cameras rolling.

He's *not* Boyle. That's the fact of the matter. He's just a poor, stupid actor who's gone out of his mind. And his madness is so contagious that I feel as though it is my own.

That's the danger and the glory of showbiz.

Not for the first time, I try to ask myself what the people out there—assuming there were any—wanted to see. Chances are good that this will be the last film, at least for a while. What would they want? If they lacked the good fortune to have a stock of Disney classics and *Lost* episodes stashed in their bomb shelters, what would they want to see from a film shot in the brave new world they'd awakened in?

If they could have the chance to choke this man, they would line up from here to Braintree to buy tickets. Fuck the cinema. Who says live theater is dead?

But they'd just be killing the messenger, once again. Missing the point, and lashing out. Just like me.

"I'm sorry," I swear to him. "Charley, I'm sorry. I swear, I won't hurt you again."

Ellison Boyle lifts his ravaged face to mine and says, in a steady *Face The Nation* voice:

"Oh yes, you will."

Then he smiles. A terrible smile.

I say, "Nice improv," shake off the implications, and guide him back to camp.

9
Production Notes

I wake up feeling perversely jubilant. Harvey is gone with a chopper and the second unit crew for at least three days.

Maybe—one can't help but wistfully add, in this uncertain world—forever.

I can't sleep on a cot. I use an air mattress on the floor of my bunker. It makes it less awkward when you need to roll into the corner and curl in a ball in your sleep. Duck and cover.

Note on my pillow. Sleeping bag imprinted by a body-shaped weight, as if someone lay beside me, watching me sleep.

BOYLE STILL A DICK, it says. MAKE HIM SYMPATHETIC.

Fuck me. Harvey hates to write as much as he loves to talk. Usually, it makes his notes bearable, but today he leaves me wanting more. I want to argue with the note, kick its ass and piss in its face on its birthday.

I could lie in bed until he comes back, let him take the wheel of this Flying Dutchman bullshit. I could probably steal some MRE's and slip through the wire, take my chances outside. I could ask Dalrymple for a job; maybe the Marines could use a lapsed Jewish filmmaker. Renounce Harvey, accept Jarhead-Jesus…

Sympathetic. Beecher has truly tapped into the withering black magic of Boyle. The footage of the boy spooked the crew worse than it did Marina and me. Not a lit major or able-bodied seaman among the crew, but anyone cast adrift long enough mutters, *albatross, Jonah, Judas goat.*

Someone's putting razor blades in Boyle's filthy new suit and boots. Every costume change, he rips himself open. A trooper like Beecher never cracks, even with blood streaming out his sleeves and pooling in his footprints. But I can't trust anyone to watch over him, can't be sure he's not doing it to himself. If I have to watch him, it's even odds *I'll* start hurting him again.

I put in a few hours with our star carnival geek after breakfast. Holding back his Dutch courage a bad idea. It took a fifth of nasty Chinese vodka to stop his weeping. We concocted a sequence of flashbacks together. Once he got the shakes under control, Beecher avidly popped into character, reminiscing eerily about Boyle's wedding night.

Boyle rattling around in a naval bunker. President's not answering his phone: ditto the Joint Chiefs in the COG fortress or the Air Force at SAC/NORAD. Which leaves him the top of the chain of command, but he can't find anyone, and the other lucky fuckers in his bunker don't feel like following orders. Still secure in his armor of denial, Boyle itches for authority, for absolution.

He turns to his wife.

And my life goes from weird to weirder.

10
The Leading Lady

Of our four actresses, only one has any perceptible talent, but I try to talk myself into using someone else.

After much soul-searching, I go to Trelawney Hinkley and take her aside.

She never had a speaking part in a studio film, but she's stunningly gorgeous and smart, and can easily evoke Mrs. Boyle's late middle-age and elegance. Trelawney probably would have been a star, if she'd let her agent change her name.

She headlined in my first indie feature, the one that killed at Sundance and got me into Hollywood. We had an affair: too wise, too complicated, to let me call it anything cheaper.

My wife found out, whipped up a hullabaloo, and used it against me when *The Indian Giver* fell through. Trelawney went off and married some TV editor. We never breathed the same air on Catalina if she could help it.

Sad, sad, hard, and sad.

But here she is again.

I have Shahmir dig up newspapers and magazines for background on Boyle's wife. A fluff feature in *Stars & Stripes*: born Olivia Wyandotte in Columbia, North Carolina; Bryn Mawr; Oxford; Yale Law School; World Health Organization; UNICEF. Marriage must've been a medieval alliance, maybe a pact to stop him devouring children.

In spite of me, Trelawney wants to do it.

I write flashbacks, set just after the bombs. Socratic dialogues make for box office death, but nobody feels like whipping up a musical number. Put Boyle's tits in the wringer. His wife wastes away. She curses him, then lapses into drugged reveries, tormenting him the most when she forgets what he's done. Finds out all over again.

Notes on my pillow, my clipboard, in my shoes, like Beecher's razors. Pearls of wisdom from the producer, left by at least one spy. Refreshing, like a steaming hot cup of black coffee in the eyes.

We find a tweed man's suit that Pierre cuts to fit Trelawney. Dowdy, but formidable; the surreal, sexless compromise left to women who wish to be taken seriously.

More scenes written, blocked out with Marina, and shot something like parts of a sort-of real movie. Without Harvey's hand up my ass puppeteering this shoot, the challenge is almost... goddamn me... fun.

***

Mrs. Ellison simmers, explodes, freezes. She drowns in her own pathos, creeping behind soothing words, a brilliant woman shackled to a shallow, unremarkable man. She begs his forgiveness for letting him become what he is. If she hadn't chased her own career to distinguish herself—if only she'd taken a firmer hand—he might have been the man America needed: the hero who could have turned the world back from destroying itself.

He rages, pleads, melts. With a White House crippled by assassins and Congress, he tried to rally the forces of good and punish the evil. It was the hardest job at the worst time, but he played the hand he was dealt, and no other man could have stepped into his shoes and done any better. No one man could have stopped it, not even one so powerful as he. Once the comm lines get fixed, she'll see how much survived, and under his leadership, the rest will be rebuilt. Together, they—

"If you have any real power, if you have any soul, Ellison... take it back. You still talk about America like it's still out there, but it's all gone. You've murdered the world, darling. Go and see what's left, and if you don't drop dead and fall all the way to Hell, you fix it, or die trying."

Exit Secdef Boyle, roaring. Exit Mrs. Armageddon, razor in hand, bound for the bathtub.

I let them try it a few different ways, but the first take is lightning in a jar. Marina smoothly steers the camera through the long single shot, so you forget you're watching through a camera.

At cut, I all but sprint to the tub—a converted men's urinal trough—to stop her.

Stop what? Stop who? Stop whatever rotten red impulse told me this film was still hungry, and Trelawney would make a hell of a meal.

Safe and sound, she sets up for the next shot without acknowledging me. She disrobes and steps into the shallow tub, brimming with blessedly fake suicidal blood.

11
Pyrotechnics

Back at the ranch, Boyle goes outside with armloads of vintage C-rations to feed the passing refugees. Shahmir wrangles a craft services station and water outside the tank traps in Company D's front yard.

We wait all day, but nobody comes. A hulking, nervy lieutenant named Salani says they've been trickling out of the hills for months as their rations run out or raiders ruin their homes. With nothing to lose, they hit the roads and sleepwalk into the city. "Everybody wants to be famous."

Salani offers to scout for extras with Predator drones. "We can pick them off from here to Palm Springs... They never see or hear the plane, man... You know what they do? They get down and pray, like to the thunder god." His smile is big enough for it to be a joke and a deadly serious fantasy.

"We don't want to shoot people..."

"No, I know..." Big Samoan smile. "Whatever... Anyway, we can bomb them with audio messages and leaflets, too. Ring the dinner bell, for sure... And if you've got the coin, you guys should totally work in the new drones, the Reapers. Sword of the Lord, dude. Dickwrinkle won't let us play with them, but if you get him to unlock the toy chest, then shit'll be on like Robotron, y'feel me?"

I back away, trying to say no with everything but my mouth. "Yeah that sounds like a hoot, but our film is a little more intimate—"

"Boring, buddy... come on, the Reapers are fuckin' sweet... VTOL-capable, full-on fighter F-42's, with sick-ass chain guns, and buttloads of tac-nuke and incendiary ordnance. They look incredible on camera, man. They can hover, and I put PA's into ours. Figure whoever'll be around will want to be able to spread the news, remind people they're still Americans, maybe draft the fit ones to kick some ass for law and order, y'know?"

Whoever'll be around. I have to piss. Beecher is nodding off somewhere, maybe trying the bloody tub, or feeding his face to the dogs. Nobody expects him to survive the shoot, especially the crazy ones who think any of us will.

Shahmir haggles with the lieutenant for the Predator sweeps, while I watch the last trace of joy in my work crumble and blow away with the wind.

11
Production Value

The crew scarecrows over to the front gates, where a semi and trailer roll into the outer compound. Harvey climbs out and pirouettes on the footrail. The crew goes wild.

Harvey makes his way through the crowd to receive the invisible baton of command. By the time he reaches me, the crew has the trailer's double doors open, and attack the cargo like jubilant army ants.

"Not that we didn't miss you," I say, trying like hell to mean it, "but what the fuck is that?"

Harvey somehow cuts a Napoleonic figure in his baggy green officer's fatigues. I wonder how long before the field promotion to Brigadier General shows up on our bill. "That, my post-nuclear scab Von Stroheim, is a fully functional location shoot rig, with hi-def cameras, editing bays, fx suites, lighting, makeup and even costumes, if you can use gold lamé togas and fishnet spacesuits."

Drool. "I salute your ingenuity. But whose is it?"

"It's mine, bought and paid for. Ask any lawyer if you can find one. You know, I lost a lot of friends and screwed some German deals when I joined that ridiculous science fiction cult, but I didn't see anybody else preparing for the future..." He dangles a big, Lost In Space-surplus prop in my face: a silver skeleton key with circuitry embedded in the teeth.

"No, you don't mean... This is not fucking happening. On top of everything else, you're one of *them*..." Even now, I dare not speak their name; somewhere out there, a robot with Gloria Allred's brain in it, or a cockroach with a law degree, is still filing libel suits for those freaks.

"No, Jesus, no!" Harvey laughs long and loud. Passing crewmembers join in. Not to make him happy; he doesn't

51

suffer sycophants. When Harvey laughs, you just want to join in, especially if you didn't hear the joke. "Those repressed shitpokers and neurotic jet-trash were dangerous idiots, but they were useful idiots. They built a bunker to store all their films, can you believe that shit? They believed their souls resided in the films, and would awaken to make new movies in their new, wrinkle-free cosmic star-stuff bodies.

"It was hell trying to keep a straight face through the indoctrination, but it was the smartest investment I ever made."

The marines crack up as they pass. Harvey turns to strut off. Over his shoulder, he barks, "Anyway. Yeah, the fucking chopper took off and ditched me out there. Do we need it today? Who cares, I feel like yelling at somebody…"

13
Character Arc

"Julian, wait!" I run after him, just noticing his queer headset. "What the hell is that on your head?" Attached to the earphone just level with his right eye, is a miniature black lens, the size of a AAA-battery.

"Calm the fuck down, Kornberg, nobody's trying to hijack your shoot. It's for the making-of-documentary. Smile!"

"Turn it off, man," I tell him with every ounce of bravado in my wiry, unworthy frame. "We need to talk about the end." I must have grown a pair while Harvey was away. I didn't fight as much as I should have. I never believed he'd ever have the resources to pull it off. I never expected any of it to come this far. I just wanted a ride.

"It's ridiculous," I say.

Harvey expertly steals the bait off the trap. "Yeah, it's gonna be awesome. You're right, we should get them started now... I've got a huge batch of old tapes, dvd's and 35mm feature reels. Most're pure crackpot shit; if any of those clowns could act worth a shit, they wouldn't need to join a cult, but there's got to be a couple hundred good B-roll sources. Tell them to start collating, and we'll meet up to refine the sequence tonight."

"But it's not just fiction! It's total buy-a-ticket-to-Heaven bullshit..."

"What was true in any of your films, Pete? Did the historical Indian Giver really sneak into that fort to tend the sick Colonel, while his people were being massacred? At least the way I fixed your script, he fought back. Humans do that. Your guy outpussied Jesus."

It's never any good to level with someone like Julian Harvey. He wants what he wants more than anyone on earth wants what's right. I argue with him here far longer than I care to record, but my best shots just tickle him. "If any people ever see this film," I conclude, "they're going to either lynch us or follow someone like Boyle, anyone crazy enough to think they're…"

"A messiah? Sure, why not? What's a savior, anyway, Pete? Only last year, a survey of schoolkids showed their heroes weren't firefighters, soldiers or astronauts. Jay-Z and Tiger Woods. They didn't save anybody, and look where they led us.

"The world needs new heroes. And what's a hero, but someone who steps into the breach to save his fellow men and…"

It's a recording. If I listen long enough, it'll just start over. So I speak.

"Boyle wasn't a hero. He's not fictitious, and he's not a messiah. You want to push it that way, fine. But the ending is like cyanide on a shit sundae. If you let it end like that—"

Harvey looks for his bodyguards, or an exit. When neither appears, he takes it upon himself.

"I have been very flexible with you up to now, Pete, because I respect your vision, your genius, whatever, and I want you to help create this film, not just ride shotgun. And I realize I'm not an easy-going guy. Easy-going guys don't produce major motion pictures.

"You can steer this film into whatever the wind blows your way. I know we can't control everything, and it's a brave new reality TV world, but I remain most emphatically adamant about only one thing.

"The ending will be finished when you reach it, and you will marry it to the film with sincerity, respect, and a loving hand.

"Or I will kill you myself, as cool and as guiltlessly as I killed your career.

"Are you hearing all this?"

I can only nod.

"I wish you didn't have to make me be such a dick about this stuff, Pete. I know everybody's stressed out—"

"Half the crew is coughing blood. The radiation—"

"Next time, let's switch, Pete. You be the dick, and I'll be the pussy."

14
Comic Relief

Harvey pivots to strut back to the trailer.

A long shadow cuts between us. A compact Hispanic private with his hair braided tight against his skull. He dances around us, babbling too fast to follow, but he gradually tunes down until his molecules vibrate at a perceptible rate.

He's holding a knife.

"Dude, you gotta put a real hero in your fucking movie, man!"

I smile and look for an officer, but Harvey chuckles, genuinely amused.

"You want to be a star, that's even harder than being a soldier, my friend. It takes more than enthusiasm to carry a sophisticated enterprise like a motion picture. What's your name?"

Redoubling his twitching, like he's trying to keep his muscles and organs from exploding out his mouth, the private barks, "Pfc. Melton Duarte, sir... but I can totally change that shit! You gotta see what I can do, man..."

I turn to walk away, douse the fire. Harvey keeps feeding it. "Well, this isn't some Chuck Norris potboiler. It's a very serious dramatic film. What have you got, Melton? Dazzle me."

"Can Chuck Norris do this, motherfucker?"

Pvt. Duarte spins and launches into a crazed kickboxing routine, kicking air so hard it should split atoms. A marine on guard duty strolls by with a well-worn *Penthouse*. Everyday oblivious.

Duarte snap-kicks him in the throat. Larynx, crushed, honks like a cracked kazoo. Duarte twists his unresisting head around to snap his neck, takes the slung rifle off his shoulder, takes the stroke mag without losing the dead sentry's place.

"Just walk away, Julian," I say.

"Pass," Harvey yawns. "What else you got?"

Duarte shoulders the gun, pivots while making the *Six Million Dollar Man* bionic noise, and squeezes the trigger.

A hundred yards away, a supply sergeant checking the unloaded truck sits down to let his brains slide out his nosehole and into his lap.

"Do you see me, Jesus? *Do you see your dawg?*"

Off the road and out into the dusty moat surrounding the camp, strutting and shouting down the barrel of the rifle, he enters the minefield.

"You think some old fuckin' candy-ass cracker *actor* could take two hours of this chicken-shit duty, you call him! But you ain't never gonna find nobody like me in Hollywood, praise His name! I do all my own stunts…!"

Pfc. Melton Duarte jumps on a mine, leaps off it like he thinks he's Jet Li—faster than time itself—and before he can hear his world go KABOOM, turns into a flock of wet, red birds that scatter to the four winds.

His rifle kicks off a shot when it hits the ground, and another when the severed finger in the trigger guard twitches its last.

Harvey bows to the crater and the gobbets of still-airborne flesh. "Private Duarte, I hope that's not all you've got, because you've left me hungry for more." Wiping bloody ash from his face, cleaning the lens of his headset camera.

"I salute your passion, but I need someone with a bit more staying power. That said, you've sure as shit earned center stage on our blooper reel!"

15
Prima Donna

The missing Chinook comes back just as the crew sits down to dinner. The thanksgiving prayer is drowned out by an ear-stabbing recording of Holst's *Mars, Bringer Of War*, circling low over the camp.

The crew runs outside, but I only have eyes for Julian Harvey, to bask in the dreamy sunshine of a moment where he doesn't know what the fuck is going on. I wish I hadn't refused my own video headset.

Lt. Salani emerges from his quarters with a squad of blood-covered tweakers behind him, looking even more tweaked than usual. The fact that almost none of them are wearing any goddam clothes at all is my first big tip-off.

The fact that they start laughing as Harvey unloads on them is a very uneasy second.

"What the blue fuck," Harvey demands, "were you clowns thinking, sending off my air support? I'm crawling around out there in a goddamned ash storm for nine hours, and you shitheads dropped me like the ugly chick at prom!"

Salani turns up the wattage on an already scary grin. "You can rest assured it won't happen again, Mr. Harvey."

"You're goddam right it won't! I don't care if His Holiness is sleeping in a coffin of his native earth, I want his…"

"What?" Salani butts in. "You want his *what*?"

And then holds up Dalrymple's head.

There's no body at the end of Dalrymple's neck. Just a couple of veins and a short stump of spine that probably stopped dripping hours ago. From the look on his poor stupid dead face, meeting Jesus wasn't all it was cracked up to be.

"Oh, shit," says Harvey.

***

Now blasting Motorhead, the Chinook touches down and throws wide its doors. We wait for colored smoke flares to pop, or a fog machine to spew clinging tendrils of mist down from the portentous doorway.

When he jumps out and shades his eyes like a men's catalog model, my mouth fills with sand.

Or so help me God, I would spit on Adrian Seele until I drown him.

Not that it would take much. Hailed as the last (and shortest) Golden Boy of Summer Box Office, Seele whored his flare for hamfisted dialogue, fascist iconography and flashy, nonsensical editing from indie YouTube videos to Sony's tentpole-dancing burlesque in four short years that seemed a lot like forever. He swiftly became the #4 director named by illiterates polled at TMZ, while toffee-nosed elitists renounced atheism to pray for his spectacular, super-slow motion demise.

His NASCAR/war epic, Yankee Jihad, *massacred the Memorial Day box office record. But clearly, the bad press never stopped going to his head.*

Born Abraham Siperstein, the writer-director-producer got surgery in Singapore to make his legs three inches longer. After his controversial, ultraviolent "rethink" of Stranger In A Strange Land, *Seele bought the rights to eight more sacred sci-fi properties beloved by the geeks who'd trashed him on the intertubes. Wiped his ass with them. And buried them in his backyard on Maui.*

Then he snapped up every award he could find on the black market and eBay—including two Oscars, fifteen Emmys, eleven Grammys, a Golden Globe and a trunkful of Ace, Essence, Espy's and Razzies (these, at least, his own)— and melted them down into a statue of a godlike hand with extended middle finger.

He rented real estate to display his self-bestowed award across the street from the LA Times, New York Times and Variety.

And I thought that fucking Harvey was bad.

"Hey, holy shit, it's little Petey Kornberg!" Seele pushes through the swell of assistants, bodyguards and autograph-hounds—including Marianne Fouts, my erstwhile makeup girl. "Jesus Christ, brother, it sure is a trip to see someone from before… in a good way, of course!"

Seele hugs me, pinning my arms before I can clock him, and kisses my cheeks European-style. Hisses in my ear, "I'll double what he's paying you to come edit for me, Kornberg. Loyalty is cheap. So is life. But in talent, you can never be too rich, right?"

"Or too thin," I mumble, eying Seele's immodest paunch in contrast to my own ribsy torso. I disengage, start pushing ahead of the entourage, eager to plug Seele into Harvey. Seele saunters along on his butcher-stretched legs, just ahead of his pack of remora.

"What're you shooting?" I foolishly ask. *And why are you still working, when there's no more Pepsi to plug in every shot, no more Army recruiters to pimp?*

Seele snorts, trying on a thoughtful face that makes his deep orange booth-tanned skin pucker like an orangutan's anus. He should have sued his plastic surgeon.

"It started out as a paycheck gig, no mistake, man… *Yankee Jihad 2*… I know, I should be excited…" I flail out to interrupt, but we're sinking into conversational quicksand. I can only walk faster. "I wanted to call it something totally different, 'cause it's not a sequel, so much as a reinvention, you know?" (Sinking…) "But Gelb and those dickless wonders at Sony think nobody will know what it is if they don't call it the same thing with a fucking 2 on the end." (Deeper…)

"My people aren't stupid like that, dude… My fans know, when they sit down in that theater, they're going to get the ride of their shitty little lives. But the point is, it's all become much more than just an action movie…"

The Marines must have turned Seele on with their super speed. All the more reason to turn him loose…

***

…on Harvey, who's got his own retinue of "buddies" from the crew. They echo and amplify Harvey's pissy peacock gestures as he circles Adrian Seele.

"What the fuck are you doing above-ground, my hacktacular blockbusting brother? I thought we WON the war on terror!"

Seele guffaws, but slaps Harvey's balding pate hard enough to leave a red handprint on it.

I have never seen Julian struck before.

"No, the war's not over yet! I'm still out there fighting it! Good to see you, too, but man, budgets are down to smash and grab, y'know?"

Julian Harvey starts to quiver with rage. And God help me, I am right there with him.

"Obtainium, dude." Seele sneers as he says it. "Whatever the Almighty gives you to shoot, right?"

"Yeah… that's right, brother," Harvey lunges into a deep yogic breathing pause. "That's why I can't help but wonder about your turning up here with next to no crew or gear, when the God Squad is still hosting our shoot."

The Marines start laughing again, and I taste ice water in the pit of my stomach.

"I mean, we're not going to be here forever," Harvey continues, a little too fast. "Believe me, they only talk cheap. And our script calls for us to bug out soon, anyway. Right, Peter?"

"Yeah, soon," I put in, desperately wishing we were already gone.

"But we're still getting the feel of a new Avid workstation, and some new graphics stuff we can't even customize yet. So…"

"So the fancy gear from the UFO cult has a steep learning curve, eh? Bummer…" Seele turns around like a football hero searching for his best girl, barking into a headset identical to Harvey's. "Wesley! Tech support! Go recon their trailer suite. Get it good! He'll figure it out in a New York mo."

"That really won't be necessary, Adrian." Harvey scans for an officer, but no eager Marines meet his roving eyes. A bunch of them cluster around us, all but chanting, *Fight, Fight*, under their breath.

Harvey's bodyguards from the island do not appear. The jaunty rapist-sergeant tips me a wink.

Harvey's brittle bonhomie fades, but his angry mask seems to be stuck somewhere between gears. What he wears now looks suspiciously like Harvey's idea of fear. "We've got it under control, man, and we don't want to cramp your style when you take over…"

"Good. See that you don't." Seele stops and folds his arms. "My people are in place in ten minutes. ISN'T THAT RIGHT, KIDS?"

"Or your money back, boss!" someone in Marine green shouts back.

The front-and-back-stabbing now in full swing, Harvey actually staggers back a step. Seele grins and closes the distance.

"You don't have to worry about the trailer and other heavy gear. Just take your people, and we'll spot you a coupla Humvees…"

"COCKSUCKER!" Harvey would sock Seele if the Marines gave him room to cock his arm. "You want us to leave now, and leave our gear—MY fucking gear– so you can finish shooting *Monkey Fuckstick 2: Redneck Boogaloo?*"

"Oh, I'm totally done shooting, bro." Seele looks like the demon he is. "Shit, we wrapped way before the bombs. But the ending was, like… times have changed, and the audience has outgrown all that *Die Hard* bullshit, right? I'm still looking for something more… you know how us creative types operate. Gotta beat the competition. And reality's kicking everybody's ass, right?"

Harvey just listens, brain-gears cranking.

"So anyway, this shit happened, so we adapted to it. Our hero had to race and fight across the desert to defuse the missiles in DC, but we tweaked it so they go off, anyway. It's fucking gnarly, but we thought, why not have it happen, and then he has to go in there to rescue his little girl, who... well, we ran out of little girls before we finished reshoots...

"So... shit." Seele's own toothless mental gears abruptly seize up. "What I'm trying to say is, I want you to be in my movie, Julian! You and, well," he looks around, "half your crew. We'll keep the computer guys and the hot chicks."

Much as I loathe the motherfucker, Harvey is not an idiot. I'm shocked to say that I almost love him, as he rallies his bluster to the cause.

"So what are we supposed to do, Seele? We don't do our own stunts around here..."

"This one'll be easy, Jules. You've got about three minutes to get the fuck out of here in those Humvees. The keys are already in 'em. All you have to do is drive and act natural."

"Fuck you in your ear, Siperstein!" Harvey's blood pressure warms the ambient air five degrees. "Salani, whatever it costs, please clip this son of a whore."

"Can't do that, man," Lt. Salani croons. "He's paying in gold and livestock. And by livestock, you know I mean bitches. All you've got is obsolete currency, lousy coke and a bad attitude.

"As for Mr. Seele... well, what can I say? I'm a fan. My brother and I signed up the day we saw *Yankee Jihad*."

16
Action Sequence

There's no time for anything but running now. Three minutes may seem like nothing, in anything but film time. But when they're all you've got, they boil down to an extremely compact forever.

Once the guns cock and aim at us, there's nothing left to negotiate. Even Harvey gets that. And God damn if that pudgy little prick is not a sprinter, as push comes to shove.

"MARINA!" he howls; and she bellows back, "HERE!" And somehow, I know that Beecher's in tow, with the camera already rolling.

We pile into the nearest vehicle, Harvey naturally taking the wheel. I think about hopping in the passenger seat, then throw that door open and urge Marina inside. She needs as much of a 360 as she can swing. And I need to be in the backseat with Beecher.

Just like that, I know what to do.

Seconds later, we are squealing on scorched pavement. I'm not sure if the Marines in front of us are there just because or on Seele's command, for entertainment value. But we plow through them all the same, on our way out the gate.

Marina, of course, is strapped in tight, catching it all through the windshield; and that's great, I hope we get to use it. She's got about one more minute to do it.

Then I'm gonna need her ass at my full command.

Because God help me, I just figured out how to direct this fucking scene.

"BOYLE!" I yell over Beecher's caterwauling, loud enough to get everyone's attention. Beecher whips around: in terror, in character, in sudden silence. Perfect.

"We're still makin' a movie, baby! And we only get one take on this shit.

"So here's what I need for you to do, and we're gonna keep it simple, okay?" Still yelling. I need Harvey and Marina to hear this, too.

"I DON'T WANT ANY MONOLOGUES! Not a fucking word, you understand? I don't wanna hear what you say any more! *NOBODY gives a shit what Ellison Boyle says any more!*

"WE JUST WANNA SEE HOW HE FEELS!"

We stare into each other for a second. I lean in, seeing exactly what I need to see.

"It's all in your face, man. It's a pure actor's moment. Just let us *watch you think*, and that's everything we need."

He nods his head. And I can hear Marina shifting in the front seat, turning, already getting where I'm going with this.

"So you don't look at me. Don't look out the window. Don't turn your fucking head, no matter what happens. Just stare straight in front of you, so the camera doesn't miss a second. And listen close.

"I'm gonna walk you through this. I swear.

"And it is gonna be great."

Beecher nods several times in rapid succession, streaming tears. Already looking straight ahead. Already deep in the moment.

I hope to Christ—a guy I've never believed in less—that Marina is on it.

When I turn to the front seat, she is.

"Just *stay on his face*, no matter what," I tell her, sliding out of camera range. "Medium close-up, till I say different. I want this much shoulders, and this much window behind him." Extending my hands, to show the perspective.

"I have him on the right, with a pretty straight shot of the road behind us. But there's a little reflection, off the back window…"

"Are you in it?"

"Yes, a little…"

"Fuck it. We'll fix it in post."

Marina smiles slightly, but Harvey guffaws. It was, in fact, a joke mostly for him.

"And YOU!" I bellow, addressing him with pointed finger. "JUST FUCKING DRIVE! Get us out of this shit, and I swear to God, I'll give you your goddam masterpiece!"

Harvey throws me a wink in the rear view mirror, keeps driving. Not saying a word.

I look out the back, see three Humvees trailing behind us. The rest of our people, also fleeing.

And deep in the distance, something ignites in the sky.

***

It's Salani's Predator drones: remote-controlled winged missiles with missiles of their own, on-board cameras to catch all the action, and blaring searchlights that bore down upon us at incredible speed.

"This is it," I say, just out of frame. "The Army you commanded is hunting you down. They have turned on your ass. And it can all end right now. And all of your dreams were for nothing. But you do not say a word."

One of the Predators fires a missile. It blows up thirty feet away from us, but I only see the flare reflected on his face as he flinches, stifles a scream.

My eyes are only for him.

Anvils of static from the dashboard HF receiver squelch out the firestorm. Ditto the twittering of the Humvee drivers on our headsets.

Suddenly, the voice of Seele dominates the airwaves.

"You know what drives me fucking crazy, though? Hey, Salani, bring the drones in tighter... Even when they give a pass to my work... shit, do I have to do it myself? Never a solid thumb's up, except from cocksucking Larry King... Lower, lower, Jesus, give me that! No, all I get is, 'It's a pretty good popcorn movie, if you can turn your brain off.' What the fuck is that supposed to mean? Which one of these arms the Hellfires?"

The melted highway before us leaps out in stark relief with the next explosion. The concussion whips us across both lanes. Tires spin on black glass.

"Shit, I thought these were heat-seeking!"

"Not from sixty feet away, they're not!" Salani, in the background, is starting to sound pissed. *"You gotta pull way the fuck back for that..."*

For just a splinter of a second, I see a Predator drone like a pterodactyl swoop between us and the next Humvee, shielded camera eyes winking.

"Awesome shot!" Seele squeaks, soaring on tweak and adrenalin. *"I mean, restaurant critics don't say, 'It's good food, if you can turn your tongue off!' When I try to watch the kind of serious, grown-up gimme-an-Oscar tripe those critics slobber all over—no offense, Petey-boy, but... MOTHERFUCK, Salani! Would you lock the fuck in? It's NOT too close, you stupid shithead! Just MAKE IT WORK!"*

And all through this, Beecher stares straight ahead, while Marina strains to hold her shot.

"I WISH I could turn my brain off, because my brain tells me those movies are FUCKING BORING! There's no clear-cut right and wrong, no dynamic tension, no conflict... no explosions..."

Harvey manages the Humvee like the formula car he tried to race in Long Beach, but he doesn't wreck this one. We lurch back in our seats, hurtling faster into emptiness.

"Fine, fuck the missiles! Gimme that joystick!"

I can barely see the Humvee behind us. The third one is long gone in the dust and ash whipped up in our wake.

Then the spotlights dip down from the right, and I hear the explosion, but what happens is a dim flash like a nebula in the rearview mirror.

"Holy shit! Did you guys see that? Oh my God, the nosecone view was priceless! The look on that driver's face... Harvey, what was that dude's name, because that was Best Supporting shit, right there."

Salani croaks, *"Dude, those are EXPENSIVE!"*

My iPad shows me the instant replay. The Predator drone kamikaze dives into the driver's side door of the third Humvee with an arcade warrior's precision. Those inside scream and die. And everything goes boom.

I don't have to tell Marina not to break off from Beecher's face. I don't think she even noticed.

That's when something drops out of the ash-clouds and blinds us from 1,000 yards away. Headlights. On an unmanned fighter jet, hovering before us.

It's the Reaper.

"STAY ON HIS FACE!" I scream, but Marina whips around. She can't help herself from getting at least one long three second view through the windshield, as we hurtle toward it.

Then she turns back to Beecher/Boyle. The raw terror on his face says it all.

Harvey neither turns nor slows down. The look in his eyes, from the rear view mirror, is undiluted by fear or despair. It's fury of the kind you only see when an A-list player gets stuck at a back table in a hot restaurant.

He punches in the button on the console that lets him yell, "I WISH YOU WERE SMART ENOUGH TO REALIZE HOW MUCH YOUR MOVIES SUCK, SIPERSTEIN!"

Seele laughs, high-pitched and crazy. The Reaper strafes the road before us with its machine guns, closing in. The warped tarmac splits like charred skin.

Beecher's eyes widen impossibly, as if to take in the fullness of God.

"DON'T CUT AWAY!" I shriek.

"I'm smart enough to know what people like, loser! They like to see the good guys win! They like to feel like they're right! Like THEY'RE the winners, for once in their lives!

"SO WHO'S GOD NOW, HARVEY? Lemme give you a hint: I AM FUCKING GOD NOW!" He laughs and he laughs. *"I've got final cut! I've got an infinite budget, and the whole world for a set!*

"The old God fucking WISHES he had the kind of power I yee—!"

Then there's a gurgle like a cut windpipe, squirting.

It takes a second to realize that Seele is done talking.

When the Reaper stops firing, lifts up and over us, I register the moment through the eyes of Ellison Boyle. They mirror my own heart-thudding relief; and what's more, my own readiness-for-death, again postponed.

It's still not over, after all.

A minute later, the headset rustles and clicks. Salani says he's really sorry, and if we want to come back, he's willing to work something out.

"And Seele?" Harvey asks.

Salani laughs, rueful. "*Dude went WAY over budget. Wasteful as fuck. No sense of perspective. Had to pull the plug.*

"*And we may not be all rah-rah God as the Colonel, but NOBODY should have to work with a goddamn blasphemer!*"

17
Regrouping

Harvey wants to go back. Some of his arguments are more persuasive than others.

We were lucky to buy back the truck, and it cost us all our cigarettes. Bao Dinh, Rob and the other techs all took shelter in the trailer when the shit hit the fan. Aside from Marianne Fouts, we left no one behind. I want to believe I would go back for Fouts, but Trelawney said the makeup artist was surrounded by horny Marines, with a pistol at her temple when the truck left the compound. Those who know Marianne say she'd never let them touch her.

Salani doesn't want to talk about her, but he says we're in the black, if we want to come back, and no more morning prayers.

Five good people were in the blown-up Humvee: Bernie Balistreri, Lalo Shahmir, Peter Hayworth, Sheila Rushkoff, and our second cameraman, Joe "Eyeball" Mamoulian. Joe's camera was running when the Predator hit them. The feed is stored on my handheld, along with Seele's nosecone footage.

I almost delete it all, but what would they want? They survived the deaths of tens of millions, but got killed by a movie.

The insanity of it all dawns like gamma rays out of their brains and flash-rots each face, as every jittering frame catches one of our dead friends. This is all that's left of them. Seele would have made them into faceless casualties to cheer and crow over, but I will try to honor their deaths, feed the audience their fear until they choke.

Maybe some of them will wake up and remember that they are human.

***

Harvey says we've only got a week's worth of water and food, a couple cases of vodka and Nicorette and a few pockets filled with the Marine's weapons-grade speed. The Colombian courage is long gone, but nobody's got the energy for withdrawals.

Beecher is a puzzle. He's a wreck, but his Boyle is uncanny, poised and penetrating. Lines scripted and ad libbed flawlessly in one take, but the rest of the time, he's weeping and raving, or morbidly fixated on nothing. Hasn't slept in days.

I followed him out into the desert after dinner last night. Concerned? Not so much. Beecher has tapped into something I would call God, if I believed in God.

Even the women are going bald, but Beecher sports a silver beard to shame Moses. So long as the guilt and rage and anguish of a murdered nation needs a lightning rod, he will be animated by it.

Maybe Beecher died days ago, but Boyle will survive us all.

Truth be told, I suspected—hoped—he was holding back some coke.

He took out a handmirror and knelt over it. I came closer, almost standing over him, but he ignored me. Scooped up a handful of fallout dust, rolled up a C-note, and snorted it.

I tried to stop him, but he would not be moved. I could not shut him up. He babbled glossolalian nonsense like Dalrymple's god-haunted Marines. But it was worse than nonsense. A million words in a thousand voices burst out of his mouth. He sang and cried and pleaded and cursed and prayed.

I don't know what possibility scares me more: that his mind could fragment so as to speak in so many voices at once, or that the cracked, empty glass of Charley Beecher is possessed by the ghost of a city.

We're all breathing it. If I let my guard down, if I try to go to sleep, I can almost hear them trying to tell me their lives.

18
Extras

And the show goes on.

We pass through a town without seeing anyone, but Harvey calls a halt. He blows up a frame on his handheld and pipes it to me. Eyes in the empty windows, uneasy apparitions in every shadow. I argue with him, it isn't there, it's a trick. We're all on the dust.

Harvey strolls out and offers vitamins, iodide tablets and MRE's for extras. I have finally worked the flight footage into the script. Boyle's escape with Sinard's deposed colonel dovetails neatly with the averted rape scene and the failed attempts to feed the passing refugees. When the colonel succumbs to radiation and dies testifying, Boyle hobbles down the road alone.

The town comes to life, if not quite alive. The people are starving, but they've found an artesian well that isn't glowing.

They've all come through the war to run out of food or lose their loved ones to marauders, and they've all passed by the Marine base, where they were offered the benediction of Christ the Warrior and a specially blessed mercy bullet.

Nothing to hope for, nothing to believe in, and suddenly, they're movie stars. Hardly all-singing, all-dancing go-getters, but they take direction well.

So here's the scene they're playing...

***

Boyle gives away the last of his rations. For a few minutes, he's pretty popular, but then someone recognizes him. Or thinks they do.

So much for the savior of our nation.

71

Over the hastily-emptied pouches of turkey ala king and rice pilaf, the survivors hold a swift trial and instant sentence. A rope of braided tire tread is hung from a playground swingset behind a burned-out elementary school.

The crowd perches Boyle on a child's desk and gathers round, as if the warmth released by the Secretary's death is the only heat left in the world.

They ask him if he's sorry.

"Yes", he says.

Tears cut through his filthy mask. A capillary bursts in his nose, adding blood to the deluge. With his hands tied behind his back, Boyle bows to the limit of the noose, choking himself as he pours out his confession.

He never let himself grasp the reality of war, because he feared it would weaken his resolve. The hard decisions he thought were easy never meant anything to him.

He believed in America as God's favorite, and never supposed the Good Lord would let them perish. He thought he was a hero when he launched the nuclear strike after the President was assassinated: a man of destiny, guiding America through another routine crisis everyone in power expected would end like all the others, with a close call and a parade.

He played dice with their lives, and lost it all. He followed orders. He didn't give his life to stop it when he could.

And for that, he is forever damned.

He prays to a raging, untenanted sky. If he could take it back, he would die a thousand times. Let his death count for something, you impotent holy bastard. Let him offer himself up for all of them. Only one man, but a mountain of shame, a desert of dead dreams, and a world of wasted chances.

Let him undo everything he was, everything he did, if it will give the world another day. One more chance to get through the day without Ellison Boyle at the controls.

Let these good people go forth and spread the word, that the monster who defiled the world is dead, and let them build a new America out of the ashes of the old.

Silence, but for faint weeping.

Then Ellison Boyle steps off the desk. He falls with his chin tucked in.

He falls, and hits the ground.

The severed rope slithers over the bar and piles in his lap.

The refugees turn and shamble away; repulsed by the enormity of Boyle's guilt and a lingering tribal fear of killing a pariah.

Boyle curls up in the dust and weeps. Completely unhinged. Unborn-again. Half-shriven.

We shoot this, of course, from a hundred angles. In the end, Marina frames him from atop the swingset, looking down on the most miserable debris in God's creation.

A dead man, awaiting rebirth in a womb of ash.

I have to admit, there's some power in the imagery.

I desperately want to believe it isn't just a huge pile of shit.

19
Mission Statement

Harvey and I, at it again. Starting with me:

"Thing I really don't get is, why?"

"Isn't it plain?"

"Oh, yeah! It's as plain as the nose on my ass! You've seen how the other half lives. How is a movie going to help them? We could go east, out of the fallout pattern. We could find a safe place to start over... Why do we have to kill ourselves to make a fucking movie?"

"Who the fuck *are* you, man? Why make a movie? Because we're alive, and *that's what we fucking do!* What the hell else are we supposed to do?"

"Live. Start over. Grow food. Make three-headed babies, I don't know..."

"I grew up on a farm."

It's all I can do not to laugh until I shit the seat of my soul. "No kidding."

"You tell anyone, I'll deny it. I couldn't grow mold on bread. But that's not the point.

"The point is: America hates Hollywood. Because you know why?

"*We came from them.* But it wasn't good."

I've got nothing to argue with there.

"All of us got beat up and kicked out of our homes for being gay or weird or starved for attention, or just hungry to do something more with our lives. And we made them feel like dirt."

"I know," I say.

"So instead of kissing middle America's ass, we told them that life on the farm wasn't a slice of heaven sprinkled with fairy dust."

"That's right," I agree.

"But they hated us for trying to warn them. And every time they lost a war, it was *our fault*, for stabbing them in the back."

"I know," I say again.

"So they hated us because we didn't tell them flattering lies. And I understand that. And I also understand your objection to telling them the flattering lies they begged for."

"Thank you," I say. "That actually almost means a lot."

"But your objection to this film has always been that it's a lie…"

"Exactly."

"The same kind of lie that got us to blow ourselves up…"

"That's what I've been saying the whole time…!"

"The kind of lie that makes them *love us*, instead of hate us. *Listen to us*, instead of ignoring us. *Pay us*, instead of letting us starve."

"Yeah. It's called selling out, Harvey. Tell me about it. Or better yet, don't. Cuz we both know that drill.

"And it doesn't matter.

"Bottom line: they hated us because we were different. Because we didn't buy into their lies, and their wrathful god didn't crush us.

"So when we come parading down Main Street—tan, fat and fake as ever—why should they treat us any better than Ellison Boyle?"

Harvey smiles, produces and lights a joint thicker than my thumb. Where does he keep getting these fucking things?

"We have food. We have hope. And we're going to make them famous."

I forget what happens next.

20
Expendables

The following day is stressful.

The two-lane blacktop meets Interstate 10 about fifty miles out of downtown LA. Scattered cars sit on the shoulders and the lanes with their doors yawning open. A tiny ghost town with looted outlet mall hugs the junction.

We hear the roar of engines louder than ours. The Humvee stops in the first intersection on the main drag, and arrows seem to pop out of its armor.

For a moment, when I see them, I'm almost nostalgic.

Motorcycles.

A gang, too many whirling too quickly around and around us for a census, but they look hungry enough to eat us.

Before Harvey can bark any orders, I jump out of the semi and walk out in the open with my hands up.

A biker with a gas mask and a suit made of plastic trash bags takes aim at me with a crossbow. The rest circle, buzzard-like.

"You guys want to be in a movie?"

***

Our little troupe has become a caravan. Word has gotten ahead of us, somehow. Every town we pass through disgorges handfuls or hordes of hungry, burned, blind survivors. *You're making the movie*, they say. Flat, hopeless faces… but a tiny spark kindled in their eyes. They don't ask for food or water, not right away.

They ask, *Can I be in it?*

Nobody seems to want to ask what we're up to, but it's all they talk about. The speculation tickles Harvey no end.

It's a latterday Bible epic, a remake of *The Ten*

Commandments; Beecher is of the bloodline of Jesus and Mary Magdalene, and is running for president; the crew is going to take the cast back to Catalina to live in paradise; in every town we've passed through, the fallout has vanished, and grass is starting to grow.

We give no comment. We feed our extras, we give them simple directions, but Beecher is our only voice. We can't become attached to these people. They're going to die here, and sooner, if they follow us. But we need them almost as much as they need us.

A few of them weasel their way into the regular crew—mechanics, cops, nurses, construction workers, cooks, a hairdresser. Many more with no useful skills turn overnight into fanatical lackeys. They quote Boyle at each other like mynah birds.

Montage fodder, set to cautiously upbeat score. I push for Mark Isham. Harvey wants Tangerine Dream, just to have something to fight over, to let me think I won. Boyle rolls into town like Hell's own Johnny Appleseed and offers cans of franks and beans, then delivers a sermon. Without preamble or apology, he tells them he destroyed America. He points to the noose still dangling from his buzzard neck, then at each of the crowd and accuses them of killing the America that could have been, and would have been, if they hadn't let America sleepwalk into this war.

"Do any of you know my name?" Slack mouths drip beans. "I was Ellison Boyle! Does that name mean anything to any of you?" Nobody knows him from Moses.

"All of you *let it happen!*" he preaches, testifies, runs rampant. "You let monsters like me run the greatest nation in human history into a grave.

"The dead are in the air we breathe. Every breath accuses us. So what should we do? What would they have us do? *What should we, the living, do?* Lie down and die? Slide into a new dark age, scavengers like worms in a corpse?

"If that is what America raised you to become, then she deserves to die. But what can you do? WHAT MUST WE ALL DO?"

His voice is a razored crow's croak, but it carries, cuts down hecklers and stuffs its message down their throats.

He commands them to go out of the cities and build new settlements in the mountains and deserts. Build a better America, this time. Never let the power to destroy yourselves fall into the hands of fools and madmen.

He blesses them and leaves, and they follow him.

He begs them to turn back. Some press unlabeled cans of food into his hands as they join the march, which he stashes until they find more survivors. *A miracle!*

Harvey provides the loaves and fishes, and even an occasional keg. He tries to snow even me that it's a miracle, but I found his survivalist Bible——a classified FEMA guide to shelters and supply caches throughout southern California.

He sends out the bikers to collect.

Our luck has been because of FEMA's incompetence at letting people into the shelters when they counted. Only a couple were already raided, and three were occupied.

One group in Pomona came out of the basement of a Methodist church to greet us, but the bikers shot them. Seemed like nice enough folks, until we saw the necklaces of teeth and fingerbones, the flyblown tunics of cured human skin.

With the other two, the raiding parties just never came back.

We have to massage the crowds so they appear to grow over his route, as the numbers of newcomers begins to drop off.

From a peak of one hundred followers, we steadily shed extras as the fallout and other, erm, hazards, take their toll.

21
Celebrity Cameo

The Puramo Indian reservation has a spectacular casino just outside Riverside: a Navajo futurist wet dream of a pueblo, dripping neon and sweeping searchlights into the sky. Two days out, we saw the dim ghosts of the lights in the fallout cloudy night, and the first roadside signs whet our appetites.

A toothless hillbilly everybody calls Gunga Din said go around it, but Harvey had to go. And I was curious.

Screaming beacons of civilization in the hinterlands of hell, the freshly erected billboards beckoned us across the desert, extras clinging to the sides and dogpiled on the roofs of every vehicle.

The world has not descended into total chaos, after all. Where the white man has fallen, the wise and righteous red man has taken up the baton. So long as they've never seen *The Indian Giver*, we ought to get along swimmingly.

Million Dollar Pai Gow, A Mile of Slot Machines, a Karaoke Contest (First Prize: A Cadillac!), $3.95 Mystery Meat Buffet, and *Four Shows Daily* by Carrot Top, Kenny Rogers and Scott Stapp.

As we close in now, the otherwise awesome Puramo Casino is indeed freeway close, but still tough to get to. Enclosed by a steel fence worthy of North Korea, a moat filled with charred cars and automated artillery batteries. We wait and wait, burning film of Boyle's begging shelter for his ragged army, but no valet comes out to park our cars.

An Escalade with monster truck tires and steer horns on the hood rolls up off the highway and honks for the drawbridge to be lowered. The extras break character to mob the spotless black luxury SUV, peering into the opaque tinted windows.

And then the inner circle of extras explodes in flame.

81

The crowd disperses in all directions, a bunch of running torches. The Escalade has flamethrowers in the undercarriage, and shoots aerosolized fire out over a twenty foot perimeter.

I saw once on CNN that rich Afrikaaners favored them for pacifying angry native mobs and carjackers.

Up close, they really work.

The ones who can still run head right into the minefield. The Marine mine that blew up Pfc. Duarte was a neutered, Geneva Convention-friendly shrapnel shredder. The Puramos clearly splurged on the nastiest bouncing-betty and daisy cutter mines on Princess Di's shit list.

Body parts fly like popcorn in a pinball machine. Everywhere they land, they set off aftershocks, until every chunk of human debris is too small to set off a mine. Clouds of blood mist hang over the field.

Alone, untouched, Beecher stands between the Escalade and the drawbridge as it finally opens.

I wish I could say I would have shouted cut, but I choke on vomit, and shooting pains down my left arm reassure me that I might just get to die of an old school heart attack.

Harvey screams at Beecher/Boyle to get out of there, but he is Moses at Tienanmen Square. He is the angel calling down God's wrath on Sodom. He is a bottomless drunken lunatic challenging a redskinned superpower with his fly open.

Marina closes in on him, skirting the edge of the swath of charcoal bodies. When she points the camera at the Escalade, the window oozes open and someone inside says something to her. She shouts, "We're making a movie, is all right with you?"

The audio doesn't come out on the tape, but her rocksteady framing shudders just a bit.

Boyle lays down in the road. The monster Escalade drives right over him and crosses the bridge, which closes.

Marina helps Beecher back to the trailer. Harvey says, "No wounded," but no viable survivors came out of the minefield, anyway.

One guy burned over seventy percent begs someone to

kill him. I won't say who finally does it.

To Harvey's credit, he doesn't try to film it.

I ask Marina what the shitheel in the Escalade said that shook her. "Oh, nothing," she slurs, clearly wanting off the subject. "He wanted what everyone wants. He wanted to be in the movie."

"Yeah, he's already in there, killing a dozen people for scratching his paint job. Why didn't you give him a fat closeup?"

For maybe the third time since I've known her, Marina shivers, wipes away tears and fights back a nervous laugh.

"It was Carrot Top," she says.

"Shit on toast," Harvey hisses. "Why couldn't we get the Gambler?"

22
Closing In

After Pomona, the pockets of survivors drop to a trickle. Where the towns once linked arms in a megalopolitan river, now it's ghost towns razed to foundations by firestorms.

We skirt the footprint of an aerial warhead detonation, huge overlapping ripples in an ocean of dust. Twisted trees of steel jut out of the waste where high rises once stood. The radiation is twelve rads.

My hair falls out in tufts on my pillow, covering my daily notes from the Tooth Fairy, who so far hasn't cashed in the half dozen teeth I've left for him. Try not to go outside more than six hours a day, but we're filming a fucking movie, for chrissakes.

I sleep in the trailer, next to the cubicle where Harvey somehow manages to get laid. Dust still gets into everything, through the makeshift airlock and into food, hard drives, everything.

Bao and Rob bitch about the dust knocking out two day's rendering work. They wear surgical masks as much to keep the dust out as to keep their steady nosebleeds from dripping on the keyboards. The climax will be spectacular, they promise. Excited, like Xmas Eve excited.

It makes me sick to my stomach. The way they talk about it, it's like they believe they're making it real. If they comp it just right, if they nail the lighting and edit it dead solid perfect, then some kind of sympathetic magic will occur.

Meanwhile, our native guides say the whole southland got creamed by about twenty warheads in aerial bursts that scoured Los Angeles County from Long Beach to Hollywood of all but the sturdiest concrete and steel buildings. Downtown took a deep surface detonation that left a crater a mile across.

The Hotel Bonaventure stood almost dead center of ground zero.

And that, of course, is where we're heading.

23
Historical Grounding

This much we know is true.

On the morning after the President was shot—the day before the war began—Secretary of Defense Ellison Boyle woke up in the penthouse suite at the Bonaventure Hotel. He had breakfast with several ranking Navy officers, FBI and Homeland Security officials, and a conference call with the new President, freshly sworn in by the Chief Justice aboard Air Force One.

The substance and outcome of the meeting was never disclosed, but those who suspect President Jim Ryan was assassinated by a cabal of zealots within the US government believe he was clued in and bought off by the successful coup plotters.

Immediately afterwards, Boyle was whisked to the roof, where he was sworn in as Vice President by Supreme Court Justice Weintraub. He then boarded a helicopter on the roof and flew to the Seal Beach naval yards, and left the United States for an unknown destination in the Pacific aboard the *USS Cerberus*, a nuclear submarine armed with seventy-two Trident missiles.

What happened next is all smoke and folklore, as foggy as the fall of Rome into the bottomless crotch of the Dark Ages. If Boyle did not launch the missiles himself, he did nothing to derail the nuclear dynamite monkey at his waffle klatsch with the President.

We can reasonably assume that Ellison Boyle never came back to America to embark upon a pilgrimage to rally the survivors and offer his life up to God to beg a miracle.

What we can reconstruct about the fate of the real Ellison Boyle is corroborated only by the video I shot that last night on Catalina.

And Harvey just asked me to trash it.

24
Montage

I'm cutting the montage—with Harry Walter, the editor, in the trailer—when Harvey comes in. The telltale green dust of Marine speed adds a festive leprechaun tinge to his red beard.

"We always knew the first act needed something," he begins. "I was really just waiting for you to come to me about it. I thought it was just obligatory…"

"To use the sack of Avalon in the movie." I look to Walter. He tries to pretend he isn't there, silently staring at the monitors. Brilliant editor; but in a fight, you'd be better off with Gandhi at your back.

"It just makes sense, man. It's the best way to honor them—"

"Are you out of your fucking mind? Were you even *there*, when they came into the harbor? Hundreds of our friends died down there, Julian. People I always wrote off as dickless went down to Avalon with whatever weapons they could find to defend our home. Steak knives. Bows and arrows. They tried to blockade the harbor with their yachts. They kamikaze bombed them on fucking Waverunners with gas and dynamite.

"Did you see any of that, from your palace up there on the hill? You had a huge party that night—"

"I invited you—"

"Did you watch the footage I shot? You took it away from me, but have you looked at it?"

Harvey tries to handle me like a starlet freaking out on diet pills, stroking my arm as if the trembling running down it is DT's and not the divine imperative to smash his silver-tongued face in.

"Okay, let's take a look."

"But if you use it, you use my cut, and no digital wizardry. I want this part, at least, to tell the truth."

He takes a tenth of a second to switch gears. The untenanted waxen mask gasping at me is priceless.

"Okay…" He leans over me to cue up a huge file on the nearest workstation.

We watch.

***

I haven't seen it since I shot it. I swivel my chair away from Harvey so he can't see my eyes. It would break what's left of my heart to see Julian's reaction to it.

On the screen…

The sirens wail just after dusk. Out on the end of the long pier with a born-again preacher and bodybuilder named Damien Fitch. A wonderful guy, totally unashamed of how he made his fortune as a gay porn star named Divinity Fudge.

He's showing me the swordfish he caught on his catamaran. It's stunted and sickly, with half its snout chewed off, but it's a milestone, the first fish worth keeping that didn't make the harbormaster's Geiger counter squawk. The deep Pacific currents out of the west are reviving, Fitch says. He swears he saw dolphins yesterday. "Somebody shut off the fucking sirens, I'm having a moment here!" he jokes.

The first rocket salvo slices through the background quite by accident. The frame goes foggy as the autofocus tries to balance the plumes of white-red incendiary fire that appear like a grove of miniature mushroom clouds along the promenade.

Flaming leaves tumble down the walk to vanish in the water. Each of them is a person I know and, with a few unworthy exceptions, love.

Damien Fitch takes up a rifle and looks around for someone to shoot. The camera jogs and jitters in a hacktacular way Seele would have swooned for. I run up the harbor to the gun emplacement at the head of the pier. The harbormaster, a colorful Aussie expatriate named JB, looks and sounds exactly like the cartoon character Dangermouse's rodent sidekick, if that means anything to you.

"Crikey! They just hailed me to enter the harbor! What did we do?"

"Why didn't you fucking warn us, JB?" A soap opera actress whose name escapes me, but who became a legend for being snubbed for two decades by the Daytime Emmys, seizes the ruddy chipmunk by the jowls.

"I had to look it up in the code books, I'm a bit rusty, y'see, but said they was the bloody Navy, din't they?"

And it is.

I pivot and back up to take in the whole harbor, just as two gnarly cyber-PT boats skate into the harbor, raking the moored yachts and motley ski boats and ferries. The light of the fires paints a Gericault panorama in Caravaggio relief, as struggling swimmers get sliced up by hooting, pimply kids in flak jackets. Siren speaker cones blaring one of Metallica's shittier later albums give a cheap action scene veneer to their massacre.

What are they *seeing*, those fucked-up, orphaned killers, that they can shoot and laugh? What happened to them out on the empty seas for six months? Are they even a Navy anymore, or just rabid killers cut loose from all the strings of their oaths, and turned pirate?

Whatever they are, we are their meat.

But not without a fight. The intact buildings up in the hills pour shouting instant soldiers down into the firefight. We had some serious militia training, before the action movie cult retreated into its compound; but aside from a few rogue assholes and a dipshit drug kingpin who swept in and proclaimed himself emperor, we'd never faced a threat serious enough to think we'd ever have to fight.

I did not fight. I watched them. I told myself later that my recording eye was the only way that anything we stood for could win. I risked my life at least as insanely as any of the people whose deaths I witnessed, but I got lucky. I am not the hero of this story. No divine hands delivered me to meet some higher destiny. I thought I was spared to tell the truth about what happened, but I was only spared to advance the plot.

It goes on and on. I skip forward through a half hour of slaughter, rapine and pillage. Sickeningly, the quaint island village setting, the smoky night sky, and the outlandish garb of the sailors evokes the *Pirates Of The Caribbean* ride so perfectly that it must be a parody, or Disney would sue.

I speed up until I see the crux of the sequence, and let it play. A low, vast black shape prowls the harbor's wreckage like a god of all sharks. But its overgrown dorsal fin is dotted with men in peaked officer's caps. They watch through binoculars, and direct a sailor to pick off targets with a 60-caliber machine gun.

I zoom in across a good quarter mile of smoky water and fires. I spent a lot on my camera. If Zapruder had one, we would have counted the fillings in the smile of the dick on the Grassy Knoll.

When the shot stabilizes to frame the three men on the conning tower, I pause it.

***

"We're not telling a lie, we're making a myth. Is that right, Harvey?" I ask him. "Is that still true, today?"

Harvey shrugs off any criticism that would wither or reform a whole human being, but he bridles at being called a hypocrite. "You know I believe in this project, Kornberg. I prepared for this! It's my fucking baby. Don't you ever call me out, or you will finish directing this trainwreck as a head on a fucking stick."

True drug addicts instinctually loathe people like Harvey, because they're a waste of drugs. They consume insatiably, but they never get hooked, and seem twice as spun sober.

What Harvey is always tripping on, I just now realize, is the dissonant brainwaves he induces in people. If a god is nothing but a monster that feeds on human worship and misery, then I have to agree with Harvey that he is indeed a god. I went to Catalina to hide from Hollywood and write something real again. I point at the screen.

"Tell me the truth, Julian. Tell me what you see."

"Bao and Rob will doctor the footage so they look like regular pirates… maybe the Cubans… or hey, how about North Korea?"

"The Navy did this. Our Navy. The clean-cut, patriotic kids who went to our movies did this to us. You want to turn it around with fancy cutting so Boyle is a victim, fine. I have plenty of footage of Beecher moping around Casino Way, mooching drinks and crying.

"But we're not changing anything else. Use it all. Raw."

"That's daring, and you know I never shy away from controversy, but the timing sucks, man, and we already had to give the Marines a black eye after that deal went sour. It's a new kind of filmmaking for a new world, sure, but I'm worried it'll start to emerge as a motif…"

He's on autopilot, feeding me the same lines he spun when he took *The Indian Giver* away from me. I wonder where the rest of his brain is.

"Look, asshole…" I take a deep breath. "I don't have a copy of *Jane's Guide to Ships* handy, but I'd bet my last solid tooth that it's the *Cerberus*. The last newscast I saw said Boyle skipped the press conference at the Bonaventure and took off from the roof. He sailed into folklore heaven on a nuclear sub. For all we know, he started the war himself.

"That is the fucking sub.

"And that," I conclude, pointing at the three men in the center of the screen, "is Ellison fucking Boyle."

The two Navy officers are all spit and polish—regulation to a tee—and would be unremarkable if one of them hadn't surgically removed his lips, and the other hadn't decided to tattoo his face like a Maori islander.

The man between them wears no uniform. His wild, shaggy hair flies up around his face in a High Renaissance halo. Clearly a man of grave destiny, the hero of a Biblical epic.

His high, peeling brow, mutton chops and bushy eyebrows make him a ringer for Peck's Ahab. But those muddy, hangdog hazel eyes, that drooping snout like Vincent Price's melting *House Of Wax* mask, the superior smirk that punctuated every congressional testimony with silent country club fuck-yous– stalk out of our nightmares about this film.

"That could be anybody, out there."

"You know it's him." I stare a hole straight through Harvey, see out the other side. "You knew all along, or else you watched my footage in the raft and slapped together this pipe dream while your crew was delousing us. Why else did you pick him, Julian?"

"Well, we had Beecher…"

I laugh out loud. "YEAH?"

"And besides, he's tragically flawed. He must have been a better man once, for his wife to have married and stayed with him…"

"We don't even know that! We made her up out of whole cloth, based on some bio notes. Trelawney…"

"Hell of an actress. I love what she does with Beecher. It has this bittersweet tone, you feel the history there, the missed chances… I'd love to see more of her, at the end, and she says…"

"Don't change the subject."

"Fine!" Harvey throws up his hands in defeat, but can't stifle a Bre'r Rabbit giggle. "You can have it! As a matter of fact… I fucking love it! The attack is a flashback, anyway, so we leave it open-ended. It's a nightmare. I love zeroing in on that other ghost of himself, the guy he was becoming. That gives you your whole artsy David Lynch doppelganger thing…"

"Or Henry James. 'The Jolly Corner,' if you want to think of it that way. Sure, whatever. Make yourself happy, in your own weird mind.

"But the way I'm going to cut it, anyone who wouldn't drown in a shower will suspect that the whole pilgrimage is a dream in the diseased brain of the *real* Boyle—out there on the high seas with his jolly pirate gang—to salve his stunted conscience."

"Fine, smartass. I love you! You make me fight, but the result is electric. We are going to knock this one out of the park, buddy. They'll have to start up the Oscars again, just for us."

"What about Trelawney? You want her in the last scene, in the hotel, right?"

"No, she's in the crater. Write her in, as Boyle's guardian angel, or something."

"WHAT?" I didn't think I could sink much emotionally lower. "So...WHAT? You're gonna comp her in with a green screen, right?"

"No, it should be in-camera, or Beecher won't get out of his fetal curl. And she's as adamant about the whole 'reality' thing as you are. Crazy fucking actresses, right?"

"You can't..." I start to say.

Julian shrugs, as if to absolve us both.

"Pete? It was all her idea."

25
Production Design

The last real sign we see of sustained human occupation is at the 10-15 junction. At its height, the swooping columns, clover leaves and flying buttresses of the freeway unconsciously described the skeleton of a fetal religion, the cult of the car invoked by roads that defiantly hurled cars into space in banked ramps that made Space Mountain look like a lame toy.

Out in the middle of nowhere, the insane concrete clusterfuck of the highway became a functional double-chambered heart, pumping cars and endless freight trucks into every capillary of America... but at night, saturated in corrosive orange lights that always seemed to burn out just as you passed under one, you held your breath like a kid passing through a tunnel, unable to put a name or a shape to the uneasy awe the junction aroused.

Someone out here saw the potential, and made the surviving pylons and marooned spans of offramps and overpass arches into a work of art. A Watts Towers for the new Necropolis of the Angels.

I've seen the catacombs under Paris and the insane skeleton-sculptures of mad Sicilian monks, but this trumps them all.

The surviving structures, every inch of them, are tiled in human skulls.

Sixty feet above the road, the severed overpasses are enhanced with artfully arranged arms overlapping like feathers, hands gripping shoulderblades in chains that actually reach out past the broken spans, extending deathgrips to almost embrace each other across the empty night.

It's so beautiful, so terrible, so epic in its scope and execution, that Dante and Fellini both would crawl out of their graves just to be a part of it.

But do we heed its unmistakable warning?

Hell, no! We've got a movie to make!

Beecher slouches under the broken human bridges like Milton's Satan descending to Hell. A grandiose self-loathing permeates every gesture. He trips on rubble blocking the westbound freeway, bows to the bridges, slams his head thrice into the concrete, and marches on.

He rails at his followers, driving them away, but he trudges on, knowing they're moths to his lethal light.

He needs them to believe, to follow.

To make his insane suicide into a miracle.

Miles of warehouses, gutted, looted. Railyards, concrete abutments sprayed with a new kind of graffiti— the silhouettes running to catch a final freight train out of the doomed city, or kneeling to tag one last wall with their initials—become graffiti themselves in as clear-cut a case of EC-Comics cosmic justice as ever I have seen.

Then, the disposable shacks and cracker-box apartment blocks of the endless East LA slums, disposed of at last: the dreams of Martin Luther King and David Duke fulfilled in a typical divine compromise.

Most of what made L.A. itself endures, though. The traffic still backs up from San Bernardino to the 101, and the bikers have to haul apart deadfalls of cars piled like leaves against the shoulders to get the truck through.

Putrid yellow-brown smog still roils overhead—forever screwed down onto the city's head by the inversion layer, like a crown of scum—but now with new secret ingredients.

Lightning stabs into the ash fields like cop helicopter searchlights. But no rain.

I don't know how long since I've slept. I feel so sick, I can't tell if I'm hot or cold. When I burn my fingers on a cigarette, it only feels interesting.

Nobody else complains.

I ride in the truck with Harvey and the effects guys. Marina and Beecher walk out on the highway. Boyle's loyal pilgrims slink along behind, as close as they dare, until he tosses another rock at them.

The iconic downtown skyline, burned into every movie viewer's mind as the archetypal City, does not tease you in from ten miles away anymore. It never bodies forth out of the murk like an imperious mirage.

It's just gone.

And that's where we're going.

26
Act Three

Ground Zero. The dirty corduroy slabs of the Santa Monica Freeway buckle into ridges and mounds of cold lava and ramparts of black glass. The jagged, jumbled landscape of skeletons and fanged spires has subsided into a becalmed sea like the one we crossed to get here.

Absolute silence. Not even weeping, as everyone hobbles into a dream come true.

Who among us didn't withhold their love for this city that made us, for hatred of all the other assholes clogging it up? You abandoned your home and old life to recreate yourself here... and every so often, the dead-eyed slut brushed away her millions of other clients to remind you why you loved her, as no other city ever could.

L.A. could make things achingly personal: taunt your loneliness by trapping you in a check-out stand behind Jenna Jameson, or put your post-divorce depression in perspective by dashing the brains out of a speeding motorcyclist across the hood of your BMW at a stoplight.

Solipsistic fantasies hold sway for the last time as L.A.'s orphan children wander into her grave. Los Angeles was our beloved whore-goddess, and she lingers on each of our heads, showing us what we wished for, all those thousands of gridlocked hours of godless prayer.

Now, at last, we have her all to ourselves.

At the Rosemead offramp, we stop and call a meeting. The crew packs into the mess tent that unfolds off the trailer. We are in the home stretch, laying the last mile of track before the grand unification with Harvey's unspeakable ending. We'll wed them together with a golden spike of pure, weapons-grade Hollywood bullshit, and then...?

The jokes about what we'll do after the shoot have worn

thin. Too many of the crew whisper about reservations at Snowbird or the Hamptons, like sick children praying in a cancer ward.

When the railroad was finished, legend has it that they dumped the superfluous Chinese coolies in Lake Tahoe.

***

The core crew and a host of die-hard extras will follow Beecher and Marina into the crater to film the penultimate scene. Nobody needed for postproduction can go.

I want to go, but Harvey overrules me. Marina seconds. I can direct them from the trailer, watching on the handheld, which will be on a hardline feed. We have a mile of cable; what luck, the crater is a mile across.

Pointedly absent from the meeting: Trelawney and Beecher.

Trelawney went from icy to liquid nitrogen after I flatly refused to let her do her scene on-location. We went outside to argue, taking weeks off our lives to scream.

I thought it was about me. She was doing this to take revenge on me for what happened before.

She actually laughed. The blood she sprayed in my face looked like scorched motor oil.

"Thank you for that, by the way." She mopped her eyes. "I never thought I'd find anything funny again. You really thought I'd kill myself over YOU?"

I should have told her, then. Instead, I let the barb dig in and ran with it. Threatened to write her out of the film. When that didn't work, I went preverbal.

If I could have shat in my hand and thrown it at her...

But that didn't work, either.

Bottom line: I didn't expect her at the meeting. And Beecher sleeps when he isn't Boyle, so I don't worry until I check his bunk.

When we're done, I deploy search parties. Harvey shrugs as we disperse.

27
Love Scene

I find a note on my pillow. Script pages: dialogue between Boyle and his wife's ghost, who takes his hand and guides him to the exact location of his suite at the Bonaventure Hotel.

She left me a video.

The camera is nightscoped. A green ghost Trelawney with spooky mirrored retinas sets the camera down on a cot, sits on a bunk beside a sleeping form, and looks me straight in the eyes.

"Pete, I know you'll try to stop me, and that you're trying to show you care.

"For the record, I thought I loved you, too. But that's not the point. The point is, I'm a better actress than anyone ever gave me credit for.

"And this is the last movie. And I'm the last star.

"And that's what this is about.

"So just sit back, and thank me, while I do what I need to do."

She looks away then, turns into Mrs. Ellison Boyle, and peels off her costume. In the harsh pseudo-light, her body still takes my breath away. Emaciated, pocked by rashes and open sores like cigarette burns at her joints, wherever her clothing chafes.

But her face is still beautiful. And her fake tits still jut in proud defiance: the last great monument to love.

She turns and leans over the sleeping form. "Wake up, darling. It's time to go."

The corpse under the sheet stirs. I half-expect her to be grudge-fucking Harvey, but it's Beecher. The sheet sticks to the oozing sores on his forehead.

"Olivia...? I dreamed... I... oh God, it was awful..."

Coughing fit shakes the stuffing out of her scarecrow. The green light glints on ropes of black drool.

She breathes deep with her eyes screwed shut, a consummate method actress, then kisses that hacking, blood-glutted mouth.

Tenderly at first, but she turns his seizure into a stormy embrace that Boyle clumsily returns. Her mouth whips aside to spit out gouts of blood, bile and mucous laced with snorted fallout, and to catch the camera's eye.

This is not for you, her eyes say. *This is for* The Day Before. *For the film. For my character. For the ending.*

I want to throw up.

Boyle recovers and stares into her eyes. "I thought I lost you... Livie... I dreamed..."

"I'm here, Ellison. I'm here, and I forgive you. I love you, honey. I hated myself for it, but I always did. You were a weak man, but you have to be strong now. You can take it all back, but you have to be strong..."

"I'm weak... sick... I can't..." A gun peeks out from beneath his pillow. "I just want it to end."

"You can't let go now. You have to go where it started. You can wake up again. Those people out there believe in you. Let their hope carry you there. Make it real. Let my love carry you."

She kisses his blistered lips, his wattled, roadkill throat. She peels his slime-sodden shirt away from his radiator ribs, and lets her tongue caress his pebbled skin, his scars, his open wounds that wink bare bone.

She takes the catch of his zipper in her teeth and drags it down.

I fast-forward through the rest.

You're welcome.

Finally, she coaxes a sickeningly enervated Boyle from his bunk and urges him out of frame.

She looks at me again, wiping her mouth, dabbing black blood out of her eyes. "I don't just want to be the last, Peter. I want to be the best."

Oh you are, baby, you are...

"We're already way out ahead of you, waiting in the crater. Try to find Union Station, because that's where we'll be until dawn. I'll have this camera, in case you chicken out. You don't have to credit me… I don't want to horn in on Marina's gig."

She coughs, catches a spray of black and wipes it on the sheets.

"You'd better start shooting now if you want to catch us."

28
No Stunt Doubles

Everybody on this fucking film is a director but me. Trelawney steered me better than Harvey ever could. She made me call off the search and roust the crew from dinner to chase her out into the crater. Not for her. I had only to see that necrophiliac mouth closing over the rancid wreckage of Beecher's organ, and erasing the disk wasn't enough.

I give it to Harvey, sick to my soul. "Another magic moment for the blooper reel. Maybe even the feature."

When Harvey says he's going out with the crew—"just to watch, you know, make sure they find our star"—I all but pack him a lunch. At last, I know this is more than a goof to him, a last chance to play his favorite head games.

We bring the truck up to a forbidding lip of petrified tsunami overlooking the mighty Los Angeles River. Once the root chord of irony in the city—a cyclopean bed of concrete and steel with huge, naked banks and storm channels (think *Repo Man* and *The Gumball Rally*)—and all to escort a miserable knee-deep trickle of industrial ooze (less than eighty percent water) dozens of miles to the oil refineries of Long Beach.

At last, the river is full to the high water mark—with carcasses of Amtrak sleeper cars and the exploded cigars of diesel engines, all mired in cobwebs and pools of glass.

The radiation is 20 rads. An hour's exposure, according to the handy civil defense bible, probably will only take a decade off the back end of your life.

About fifty feet west of us, the outer ridge of the crater drops nearly a hundred feet, and the radiation is like the heart of an invisible volcano.

Bao and Rob argue about the megatonnage involved, float a betting pool.

Marina, Harvey, the skeleton crew and the camp followers set out after Boyle. In the lead, a gangly freak clad in pigeon carcasses poses as a hood ornament, pointing the way with one feathery claw.

Harvey pulls some strings. Bikers will pick the crew up and charge down the plunging obsidian walls of the crater, paying out shielded cable from a spool in its own little U-Haul trailer.

My second unit catches it all. Crying, hugs, curses, a Gatorade and champagne toast and a toke off a fatty containing the last Jamaican Blue Mountain sinsemilla in L.A.

When he gets over his whooping pot-cough, Sinard—promoted to key grip for the day—observes that when they finish the film, he'd like to rediscover and colonize Jamaica. "Do it right, this time." Bits of lung in his smile.

Retreat to the command post, mission control center for the first manned mission to downtown L.A. The camera feed jounces and bounces on the big editors' monitors. Marina giggles.

Harvey's note on my handheld: ONE TAKE.

29
Grand Finale

They catch up to Beecher in the car-choked arroyo of the Harbor Freeway, in the lees of the shockingly durable L.A. County Jail. He doesn't know where—or who—Trelawney is. "Olivia…" he moans. "She's out there…"

Refusing a sip of water, he lurches to his feet and stumbles off to the west.

Hunks of slag and blobs of unrecognizable ruin break up the radiating pressure ridges gouged into the earth around ground zero. That's where the city we loved transformed into liquid, into plasma vapor. A gift God took back.

The crew leaves the bikers behind. One of them just drops dead across the bars of his hog as they roar off. The superstitious bikers honk their horns until they fade to silence.

Bao and Rob have settled on a thirty-megaton surface burst, and paid off the big winners of the pool.

Boyle soldiers on for about a half hour, covering less than two hundred yards, before falling and staying down. He vomits on himself. Something hefty enough to distort and darken the seat of his pants takes the back exit. He waves away the extras, reaches out for someone only he can see. "Olivia…"

"I forgive you."

The words carry on the wind, or maybe I'm the only one who hears them. Marina whip-pans to frame Olivia Wyandotte Boyle.

She looks pristine. Aglow, and not just because of the radiation or the tortured red sunset haloing her head. She beckons to Boyle through the blowing dust, and mouths the words.

I know she's there, from the eyebrows up, but I see the

greenscreen lines, and the wavering, heat-haze distortion of the screen gives away cheap effects. She's right here in the trailer…

But she's there. Bao and Rob look perplexed when I accuse them of comping a tape in over the feed.

She comes and takes Boyle's hand and lifts him up. They walk together over a hill of sizzling metal that might be pure gold, and fade out of sight.

Marina follows them. Boyle kneels on the ridge above a canal of melted traffic where the Bonaventure Hotel once stood. He waves back the pilgrims, tells them to go and spread the word. There is no promised land, unless they keep the promise themselves.

She gets the shot. Boyle offers his life up for the world he took away, for just one day, to live again, and maybe save themselves. He wheezes and collapses convincingly.

Marina lingers on his unbreathing form for a full minute. In the whipping dust of the blurry background, I think I see Trelawney turn away and hobble off, vanish.

I shout for someone to go after her, but the channels are roaring with static screams.

At last, Harvey yells cut. Just before it goes to static, I see Boyle roll to his knees and rise with almost a bounce in his step. "Let's get this execution over with, shall we?"

They can't find Trelawney.

30
Fixing In Post

I wanted to shoot the final scene before we went in, but Beecher/Boyle refused. He comes out of the crater on his feet and tells us to get good and god-damned ready to shoot the scene right away, because the soles of his feet have sloughed off in his boots, and he keeps slipping in blood.

Some of our nonunion refugee contractors built a convincing California king bed with a barely-charred headboard and nightstand, and Sinard stitched up a bedspread and curtains out of UFO togas. We cobbled together the room itself from long static shots from *The Shining* (suitable, considering how shamelessly Harvey's scene rapes the end of *2001*), and some piece of indie junk called *Conscience*.

Beecher lies on the bed. He gets up and goes across the room like Scrooge on Christmas morning. He throws open the drapes and stands agog... horrified.

Bitterness erodes his moribund face. But then, as agonizingly slow and as radiant as the newborn sun, marvels at the swelling blast of white morning light.

He smiles.

It worked...

But it's not kosher for Moses to enter the Promised Land, is it? He grips his enfeebled heart and sinks to the floor, dying in the blessed glow of that light he stole away from the world, but now has restored.

He dies, and the world begins another day.

Beecher's ulcerated face is so cratered that his teeth show through his left cheek, and his nose is all but totally gone. Our pickup makeup artist—a mortuary cosmetologist before he started singing in some godawful huge rap-metal band—sculpted a nifty fake nose out of putty, but there's barely enough flesh to glue it on.

Rob sneers at the live feed. "No problem. I can comp his

111

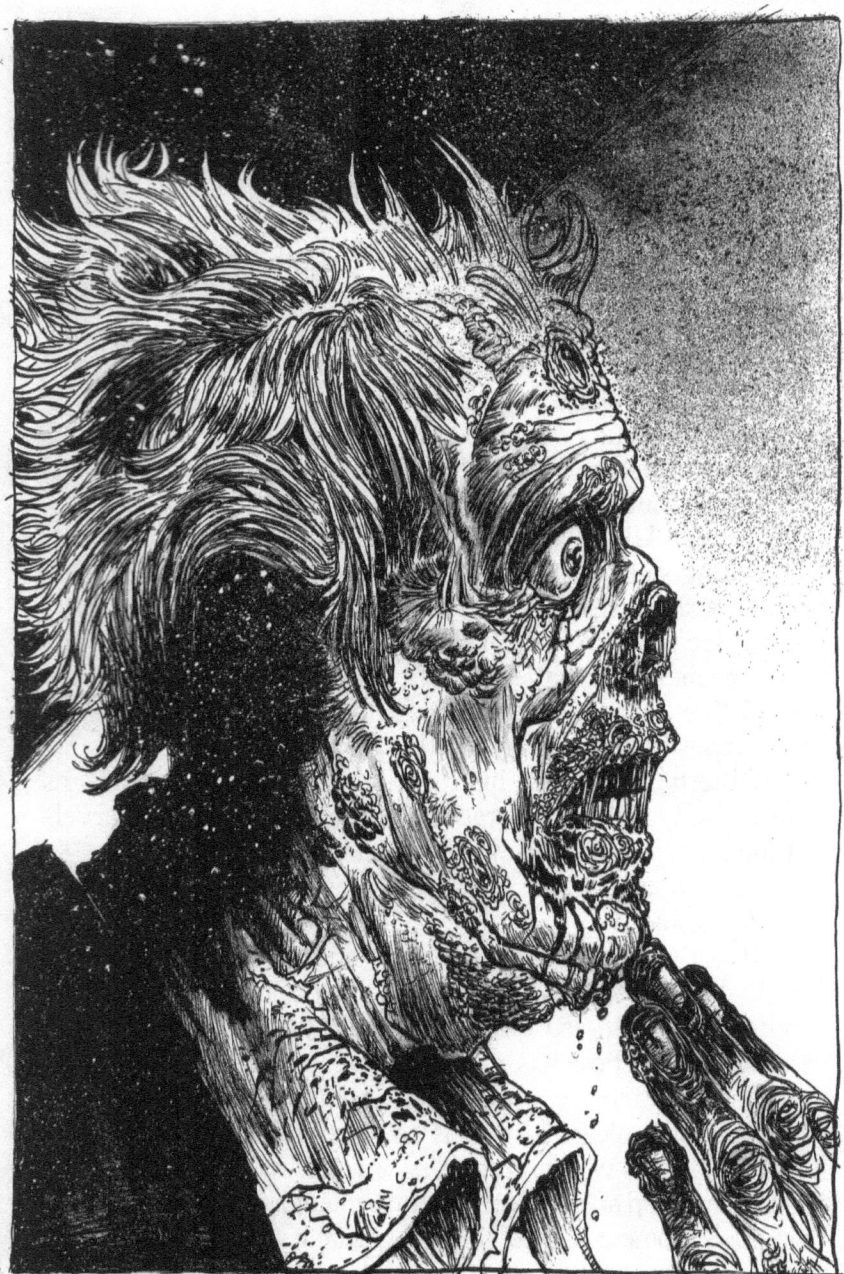

face in from the first shoot, or one of his old movies."

I figure it's already been raped, so I let him use a clip from my Catalina reels. Beecher in a drunken rant—about Ellison Boyle, fancy that—at a party on Peter Guber's yacht (always the best parties, because Guber was in Miami on the day of).

We share another toast upon their return. Sinard throws up a lobe of lung in his cup. Three extras died on the return hike. The rest stand around with their glazed eyes like ashen sunflowers, following whomever they think is in charge of feeding them, like Chernobyl chickens. Even me. They don't realize this is the wrap party.

Beecher wanders off into the dust sometime late in the party, never to be seen again.

Harvey doesn't. Instead, he strips off his fatigues in the trailer; and lo and behold, he's wearing some kind of armored spacesuit underneath. My eyes bug at the sight. I'd thought he just gained twenty pounds, like everyone else who got invited to parties on Catalina.

"What the fuck is that?"

"Russians made it for the cosmonauts on Mir. Lead longjohns, but there's a lot of rocket science in it. You get one when you go up in the shuttle."

"You never went up in the shuttle."

"The Russian shuttle, nimrod. I didn't do it to get attention…"

"What, pray tell, does your cosmonaut union suit do, besides make you impervious to shame and criticism?"

"Honestly, Pete, if I had more than one, you'd be top of my list. I need you around, man! This isn't the last film… it's the first! History's going to record that we rebuilt Hollywood with this movie, and we ruled the new America by creating its folkore, shaping their dreams."

I stand there with my mouth hanging open.

"Don't try to make me feel bad for not sacrificing myself. I offered it to Beecher, but he turned it down. Crazy fucker. But he came through, didn't he?"

"I—I just don't even know what to say."

"Then do me a favor, and don't say anything. At least not 'til you see the climactic montage."

31
The Money Shot

At long last, the golden spike is driven, and we all get to see what Boyle sees before he dies.

Bao and Rob crack open a bottle of champagne and toast each other. The sequence rolls.

***

The ground zero panorama seethes in fallout smog. Shot from the west rim of the crater, Bao and Rob recalibrated and squashed the perspective to catch exactly the view from Boyle's Bonaventure suite. Ritual magic, their quizzical faces tell me, was supposed to work wonders.

Radioactive mist streaming up out of the blasted ground pours forth into the sky like fire in reverse and congeals into columns, flows out to gel into streets and sidewalks, oozing over the jumbled Martian plain and filling the molds—one shape at a time—of ghosts.

The fog does not simply roll back to reveal the new Oz, but it glistens like the raw essence of unfulfilled promises that L.A. dripped into our junkie souls, bubbling up like Jed Clampett's oil strike and clothing the skeletal whore-goddess with a flesh of pure dreaming.

The yawning trenches of freeways birth themselves into honking, idling life, brimming with traffic. The skyscrapers of the banks and the brokers and the media tycoons who rule their corners of America like medieval Spain greet the triumphant rays of the rising sun and shine like the financial rookeries of the Heavenly Host.

The camera leaps out into space and swoops dizzily over the automotive maelstrom, soars down the teeming avenues between mushroom clouds that become glass and steel towers.

The hand of creation ripples out from the Bonaventure like an artist flooding a blank page with unflinching detail: from the armadas of shopping cart-pushing vagrants to the rooftop heliports, gardens, swimming pools and putting greens—where the rich and famous try to make their slice of L.A. a planet unto itself—with all the many millions of nobodies in between.

The smog settles down out of the sky and gushes out of fissures in the earth, and congeals into the tourist trap ranchero of Olivera Street, the riotous sweatshops of the garment district, the monoxide-trap ice tunnel of the 3rd Street underpass, the noir cathedrals of the Bradbury Building and Union Station.

And out of the twinkling, new-minted dream city come people to greet the day.

Cops, tycoons, gangbangers, teachers, surfers, bikers, actors, insurance salesmen, unemployed single moms and even a lawyer or two step into the sun, and smile.

*In dazzling mosaic sequences, we seem to look all of them in the eye. A good day, a bad day, a fearful day or just more of the same shit: in every eye, I swear those crass bastards managed to digitally insert a spark that says that—in the back of their minds—*they know *today is not just another day.*

It may be the last, or the first. But they awaken and set out to meet this day, to ride, drive or drag it through the wall into another world where L.A. will never stop turning tricks, and never, ever die.

The piss-yellow smog flows out to become the rugged green palisades of Griffith Park, its tits-on-a-boar observatory. The Hollywood sign rears up out of the riven hills of ash, over the awesome empty plains reshaping themselves now into the infinite sprawl of the reincarnated city.

The glorious kingdom that bullshit made sparkles under a pure blue-pink sky. The air's so crisp and clear, you hi-def viewers can still see stars.

We see Venice and Santa Monica, the polluted ocean

under siege by armadas of happy lotus-eaters, and I'm not the only one in the room who chokes up.

Among the hordes enjoying their last day on the beach, Bao and Rob have ingeniously comped our friends from Avalon into the picture. I swallow gum I wasn't chewing when I see Trelawney Hinkley, quite unrecognizable with her red hair down and a diver's mask and snorkel over her face. Just a few frames, as she waves and dives off the deck of a yacht.

Damien Fitch mugs and grins beside the sport fishing dock at Marina Del Rey, his arm around Bruce, the shark from Jaws.

We all see everyone we knew and lost.

It seems to go on and on, but the counter marks only sixty seconds from the framing shot to the closer: an extreme closeup on Boyle's dying eyes.

In them, we see something like a soul come unknotted from his body, and shed the weight of this life. Bao and Rob swear they did nothing to this shot, and yet we all see it.

Even if they only have a day—even if the bombs still go off tomorrow—he has saved them today, and delivered himself.

And that's how the movie ends.

And I know it's complete and total bullshit. And I know that once I step out into the sick yellow sunlight, the broken world will still be there. And I don't even know if anyone's left to see this thing, out there in the ruins of America.

But I'll kill anyone who wakes me up from this.

That, my friends, is the power of film.

JOHN SKIPP is a high school dropout turned New York Times bestselling novelist. He has written sixteen books and edited fifteen more, drafted scripts for Freddy Krueger and a singing penis, not to mention blah blah blah. But what he really likes to do is direct. His latest book is *Sick Chick Flicks*. He lives in Eagle Rock with his dog and bongos.

CODY GOODFELLOW went to UCLA to study film; after a week of exposure to the film industry, he changed his major to English Lit. He has written three novels with John Skipp and three novels without John Skipp. His latest collection is *All-Monster Action*. He lives in Burbank with his wife and two daughters.

GREG HOUSTON was born and raised in Baltimore, MD. After graduating from Pratt Institute in 1988, he left New York to return to his hometown where, with the help of two evil sock puppets named Carl and Doug, he's been happily illustrating ever since. When not engaged in a knife fight or starting random fires, Greg can be found rooting on the Orioles with his wife, Tracy, and their two mostly unlovable cats. He's also been known to skulk about the halls of the Maryland Institute College of Art where he's an adjunct professor teaching illustration in its various sundry forms.

BIZARRO
BOOKS

ERASERHEAD PRESS

LAZY FASCIST

Your Major Resource For The Bizarro Genre

WWW.BIZARROCENTRAL.COM

IN HEAVEN,
EVERYTHING IS FINE
Fiction Inspired by David Lynch

Thomas Ligotti
John Skipp
David J
Ben Loory
Nick Mamatas
Blake Butler

Edited by Cameron Pierce

For over thirty-five years, David Lynch has remained one of the weirdest, most challenging and provocative filmmakers. From his early experimental films created as an art student in Philadelphia, to his foray into digital film with *Inland Empire*, Lynch's filmography is as diverse as it is influential.

Featuring Thomas Ligotti, David J (of Bauhaus), Ben Loory, John Skipp, Kevin Sampsell, Blake Butler, Nick Mamatas, and many others, *In Heaven, Everything is Fine: Fiction Inspired by David Lynch* is a tribute to one of the greatest filmmakers of all time.

Haunt is a tripping-balls Los Angeles noir, where a mysterious dame drags you through a time-warping Bizarro hall of mirrors. She's the girl of your dreams. Too bad she's dead. OR IS SHE? In Haunt, "you" are the hapless corporate tool and rock star wannabe turned private Dick. Here, even your most inconsequential choices can make all the difference between a Hollywood ending on the beach and sucking cock for clues. This is genial lowbrow high lit weirdness: the funny, punchy cousin of Danielewski's *House of Leaves*, a Vonnegut and Salinger paté on a choose-your-own cracker, with a lapdance from Nancy Drew. As much fun to make as it is to eat!

Laura Lee Bahr is an award-winning indie actor/playwrite/screenwriter with a gift for the hilariously, tragically absurd. *Haunt* is her first novel.

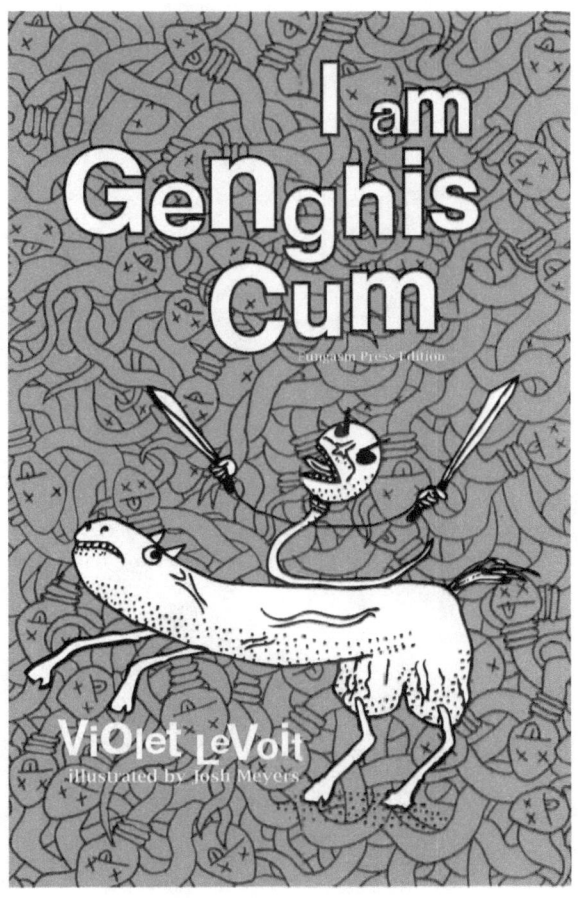

HOLY FUCK ON WHEELS! Want to populate the world in your own image, one rampaging sperm bank jack-off at a time? Would you like your stigmata with special sauce, in a fast-food corporate nightmare of hellish proportions? From the savage Arctic tundra to post-partum mutations to your missing daughter's unmarked grave, join visionary madwoman Violet LeVoit in this non-stop eight-story onslaught of full-tilt Bizarro punk lit thrills.

"So scary it's funny, so Mensa-smart it's insane, I Am Genghis Cum wants to impregnate your brain-womb and force you to deliver the unthinkable yourself. I am stunned by how good this book is."

—John Skipp, from the introduction

SO YOU THINK YOU KNOW HIPSTER HELL?
LET MAX APOCALYPSO BE YOUR GUIDE!

Los Angeles may well be the City of Dreams, but there's no denying that a lot of them suck. And while celebrity flame-outs keep us all entertained, that's just the tip of the nightmare iceberg. Underneath lie darker things, struggling to be born, and demanding their hideous shot at the top. So when two young badass women make the scene at an insane Charlie Sheen-based art exhibit, their Friday night of mind-warping horror is only beginning.

Introducing FUNGASM QUICKEES! A new line of quality subversive short fiction, gleefully busting down the pop culture boundaries at 99 cents a pop!

IT'S THEIR WORLD... NOW GET THE FUCK OFF!

The world gave him a blank check and a demand: Create giant monsters to fight our wars. But Dr. Otaku was not satisfied with mere chaos and mass destruction. Even as his subversively delicious kaiju creatures undermined the very fabric of American life, he hatched a scheme to animate the cities themselves and inaugurate a new dark age of mega-monster abominations who would finally give humanity the ass-whipping it deserved. Now only one man, riding inside the skull of a much larger man, stands between us and the planet-devastating madness of ALL-MONSTER ACTION!

"A tour-de-force! Goodfellow's latest is his best yet. Compulsive, breakneck reading!" -BRIAN KEENE, author of *The Rising* and *Ghoul*

ZOMBIE MUNCHKINS! TURD-FLINGING FLATHEADS! EVIL CORPORATE CONSPIRACIES! DELICIOUS MEXICAN FOOD!

OZ IS REAL! Magic is real! The gate is really in Kansas! And America is finally allowing Earth tourists to visit this weird-ass, mysterious land. But when Gene of Los Angeles heads off for summer vacation in the Emerald City, little does he know that a war is brewing...a war that could destroy both worlds! This loving Bizarro tribute to the great L. Frank Baum is an action-packed, whimsically ultraviolent adventure, featuring your favorite Oz characters as you've never seen 'em before. Let super-hot warrior sweetheart Aurora Quixote Jones take you on a guided tour of surrealist laffs, joy, and mayhem, with more severed heads than Apocalypse Now and more fun than a barrel of piss-drunk winged monkeys!

After the apocalypse, three Star Trek fans and their morbidly obese cat embark on a quest to save their beloved idol, the one and only William Shatner, from the hostile world America has become. But their journey will not be easy, for the wasteland is filled with cannibal cults, Klingon biker gangs, Zombie Borg, and all manner of mutant creatures. And once they arrive at their destination, they discover that William Shatner has been transformed into Shatzilla - a giant 100-story radioactive monster hell-bent on destroying all of Los Angeles. Now instead of saving Shatner from this new apocalyptic world, these three fans must save the world from this new apocalyptic Shatner. If only there was another giant monster who could take him down...

Friday the 13th meets Visitor Q. *Apeshit* is Mellick's love letter to the great and terrible B-horror movie genre. Six trendy teenagers (three cheerleaders and three football players) go to an isolated cabin in the mountains for a weekend of drinking, partying, and crazy sex, only to find themselves in the middle of a life and death struggle against a horribly mutated psychotic freak that just won't stay dead. Mellick parodies this horror cliché and twists it into something deeper and stranger. It is the literary equivalent of a grindhouse film. It is a splatter punk's wet dream. It is perhaps one of the most fucked up books ever written.

If you are a fan of Takashi Miike, Evil Dead, early Peter Jackson, or Eurotrash horror, then you must read this book.

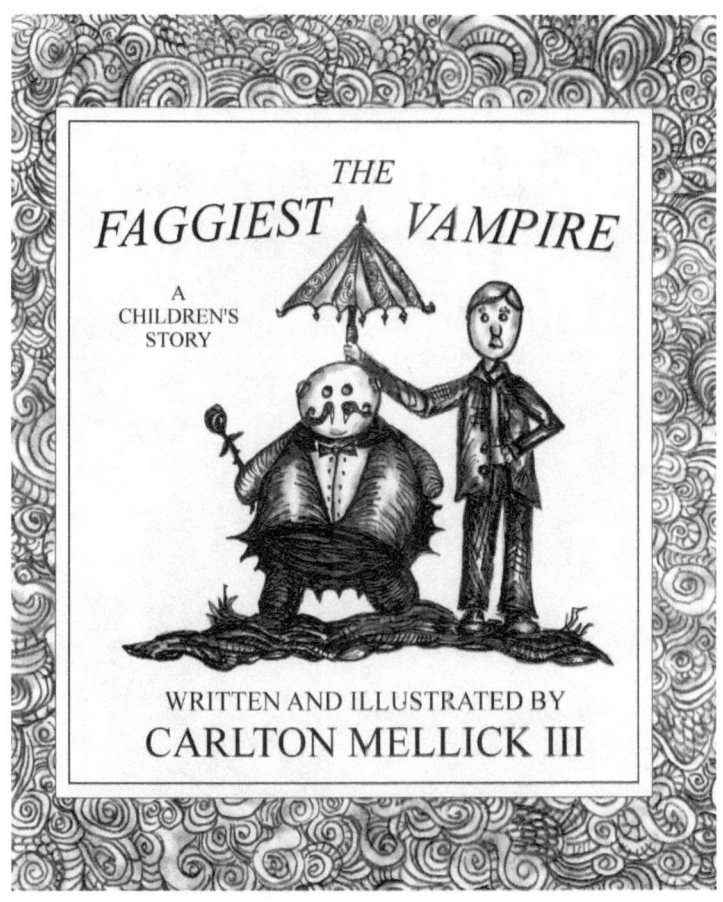

THE
FAGGIEST VAMPIRE
A
CHILDREN'S
STORY

WRITTEN AND ILLUSTRATED BY
CARLTON MELLICK III

Deep in The Land of Broodsarrow, just outside the village of Gneirwil, and high on a cliff overlooking the Everbleed Sea, there stands the faggiest gothic castle that any mortal being has ever seen. Living in this ancient faggy castle is none other than the well-renowned vampire, Dargoth Van Gloomfang. The citizenry of Broodsarrow sure has its share of faggy vampires, but old Dargoth has always been by far the faggiest of them all. That is, until a new vampire came to town. A younger, hippper vampire. One that emits such a grand amount of fagginess that one cannot help but be completely overwhelmed by his presence. Now Dargoth Van Gloomfang must figure out a way to out-shine this young newcomer if he wishes to ever reclaim his throne as . . . the faggiest vampire.

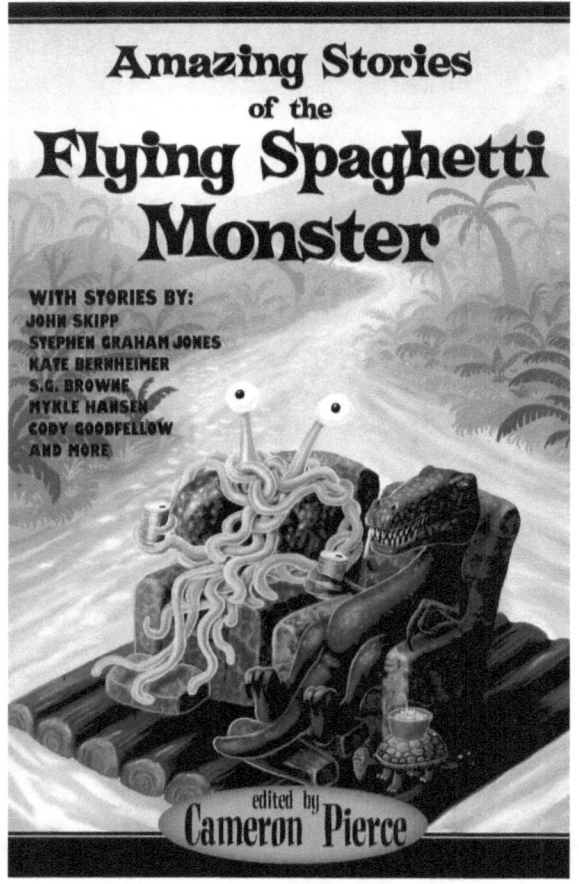

In Amazing Stories, the Flying Spaghetti Monster goes on trial to earn his godhood among a council of deities that includes Jehovah, the Buddha, Ganesh, Cthulhu, and Charlie Sheen. He is interviewed for an exclusive episode of the celebrity talk show In the Monster's Studio to discuss his relationship with Godzilla and other famous monsters. He rears his head at an archeological dig in a desert wasteland and dines with a horde of food demons in Hell. He rescues pirates, authors, and prisoners from the cold hand of death while banishing children to suffering and starvation. He is a just god, but only if you compliment his vodka sauce. Like an all-spaghetti evening of Adult Swim, *Amazing Stories of the Flying Spaghetti Monster* will show you the many realms of His Noodly Appendage. Learn of those who worship him and the lives he touches in distant, mysterious ways.

Meth-heads, man-made monsters, and murderous Neo-Nazis. Blissed out club kids dying at the speed of sound. The un-dead and the very soon-to-be-dead. They're all here, trying to claw their way free. This is a place where self-discovery involves scalpels and horse tranquilizers; where the doctors are more doped-up than the patients; where obsessive-compulsive acid-freaks have unlocked the gateway to God and can't close the door. This is not a safe place. You can turn back now, or you can head straight into the heart of...the ANGEL DUST APOCALYPSE

"A dazzling writer. Seriously amazing short stories--and I love short stories. Like the best of Tobias Wolff. While I read them, they made time stand still. That's great."
    —CHUCK PALAHNIUK, author of Fight Club